Tuesday, May 22, 1990
West Berlin

IF we had known it would eventually involve the KGB, the French National Police, and the Supreme Allied Commander in Europe, we would have left that body in the river and called the Polizei like any normal German citizen; but we were Americans and addicted to solving other people's problems, so naturally, we got involved.

Also by Rosanne Parry

Heart of a Shepherd

SECOND
Fiddle

Rosanne Parry

A Yearling Book

Text copyright © 2011 by Rosanne Parry
Cover art copyright © 2012 by Random House, Inc.
Map copyright © 2011 by Luiz Vilela

All rights reserved. Published in the United States by Yearling, an imprint of Random House Children's Books, a division of Random House, Inc., New York. Originally published in hardcover in the United States by Random House Children's Books, New York, in 2011.

Yearling and the jumping horse design are registered trademarks of Random House, Inc.

Visit us on the Web! randomhouse.com/kids

Educators and librarians, for a variety of teaching tools, visit us at randomhouse.com/teachers

The Library of Congress has cataloged the hardcover edition of this work as follows:
Parry, Rosanne.
Second fiddle / Rosanne Parry. – 1st ed.
p. cm.
Summary: Six months after the fall of the Berlin Wall, three eighth-grade girls living on an American military base with their families in Berlin try to save a Russian soldier, who has been beaten and left for dead, by smuggling him to Paris, where they are going to perform in a music competition.
ISBN 978-0-375-86196-3 (trade) – ISBN 978-0-375-96196-0 (lib. bdg.) –
ISBN 978-0-375-89350-6 (ebook)
[1. Runaways–Fiction. 2. Soldiers–Fiction. 3. Music–Fiction. 4. Paris (France)–History–1958– –Fiction. 5. France–History–1958– –Fiction. 6. Berlin (Germany)–History–1945–1990–Fiction. 7. Germany–History–1945–1990–Fiction.] I. Title.
PZ7.P248Se 2011 [Fic]–dc22 2009033324

ISBN 978-0-375-86166-6 (pbk.)

Printed in the United States of America

10 9 8 7 6 5 4 3

First Yearling Edition 2012

Random House Children's Books supports the First Amendment and celebrates the right to read.

For my mother, who taught me to read, and my father, who got me a violin, and for both of them together, who believed I could make music on the page and in my life

1

Tuesday, May 22, 1990
West Berlin

IF we had known it would eventually involve the KGB, the French National Police, and the Supreme Allied Commander in Europe, we would have left that body in the river and called the Polizei like any normal German citizen; but we were Americans and addicted to solving other people's problems, so naturally, we got involved.

It began like every Tuesday afternoon. All the other kids from the American school on the army base at Zehlendorf went to the gym or the after-school matinee or the Scout meeting at the community center, but Giselle and Vivian and I took the S-Bahn to our music lesson in downtown West Berlin. Ordinarily, as soon as we found seats on the train, Vivian would get out her geometry book and Giselle would disappear under headphones with a new cassette from the latest girl rock star. If she remembered to bring extra headphones, I'd listen along, but usually I worked on writing my own music: minuets for the violin, mostly. Not nearly as hip as "Girls Just Wanna Have Fun," but I had to start somewhere, and classical music was what I knew. Not that I'd admit this to just anyone, but classical music was what I loved–more than anything.

We were only five days away from the big Solo and Ensemble Contest in Paris. We'd been working on our competition piece, Pachelbel's Canon, since Christmas. Our music teacher thought we had a shot at first place in the twelve-to-fourteen-year-olds group, and Giselle's dad, General Johnson, had bragged to the entire brigade that we were going to clean up, so no pressure or anything. Not that I didn't love winning, but for me the big deal was that it was our first trip to Paris, and it would be our last time ever to perform together as a trio before the army moved Giselle and me back to the States.

So this time, Vivian and Giselle were listening to the Canon together on her Walkman. Vivian closed her eyes and hummed her part, and Giselle ran the fingerings of the tricky section with all the sixteenth notes. A German lady and her kids stared at us like usual. I used to think it was because Giselle was really pretty and kind of hard to miss because she was so tall, but after three years of riding the commuter train, I knew better. I'd never seen a black kid on the train; plenty of Turkish girls, but nobody as dark as Giselle.

We hopped off at the Potsdamer Platz and walked away from the park and museums and into the neighborhood of Kreuzberg, where our music teacher lived. We went right past Checkpoint Charlie—that guardhouse of Communism between the Soviet Union and the West. It was empty and dark as we walked past, abandoned as abruptly as the East Germans had voted out the Communist Party a few months before. The souvenir collectors and reporters had left months ago. Occasionally, we saw a few eager tourists chipping away at the sections of the Wall still standing, but today, nothing.

"So, Jody," Vivian said, "what do you want to see in Paris?"

"The Eiffel Tower," I said automatically. I loved tall things: roller coasters, bridges, the Statue of Liberty, the Space Needle. The upside of being a military kid was that you got to see a lot of cool places. The downside was that every time you made a friend, you had to move away.

"The Eiffel Tower? No way!" Giselle called over her shoulder. As usual, she was a half dozen strides ahead. "Everyone sees the Eiffel Tower. Boring! Let's go to the Racine Club."

"Where?" I said.

"It's a fencing school. The best one in all of France. My fencing master trained there, and he said he'd set up some bouts with the kids who are in training. Come on, it'll be fun!"

I watched one of Giselle's fencing matches last year. Right away I could see why fencing is not a sport on TV.

"Hello?" Vivian said. "This is Paris we're talking about—art museums? Ballet? Neither of you wants to go shopping?"

I, captain of the fashion clueless, shrugged.

"Let's see," Giselle said, turning to face us and extending

3

both hands to weigh the options. "Shopping for fluffy, fruity-smelling French things or meeting Olympic-level athletes—tough call."

Giselle put her hands on her hips and looked down at Vivian, which is not hard even for me. Vivian was the size of your average fourth grader. Vivi glared right back, but it didn't have quite the same punch with her preppy girl clothes and Clark Kent glasses.

"How about this," I broke in as we rounded the corner and came to our music teacher's apartment house. "There's shopping on the Champs-Élysées, right?"

Vivian nodded and held open the door.

"Then we can go to the Arc de Triomphe at the end of the street—that's famous and tall, but not so dorky as the Eiffel Tower, okay?"

Giselle nodded and pushed the button for the elevator.

"And Giselle can, umm . . ."

"Stab anyone who tries to pickpocket us?" Vivian offered.

"Exactly!" I said. "You can stab them fifteen times if you like," I added, remembering how many touches made a match in fencing.

"Perfect!" Giselle said. "And while I go to jail, you two can go see a nice fluffy French ballet." She hip-checked Vivian into the elevator as the door slid open and tugged my pony-tail as she followed me in.

"I would bring you cake if you were in jail," I said.

"Yes," Vivi added. "Chocolate cake with a bomb inside and directions for your escape in secret code!"

Vivian has read way more spy novels than is normal for a girl our age. The elevator stopped on the fourth floor, and we went two doors down and knocked.

"It's all settled then," Giselle said. "Herr Müller will be so glad he agreed to chaperone this trip."

Herr Müller met us at the door and shook our hands, just like he had every Tuesday afternoon since we were ten.

"Guten Tag, Fräulein Field," he said, and gave my hand a firm shake for three ups and downs.

"Guten Tag, Herr Müller," I said, just like I had every week. Vivian and Giselle followed me in.

"Fräulein Armstrong, Fräulein Johnson," he went on, as formal as ever. It was like meeting the division commander. We filed into his apartment looking for the usual chairs and music stands crowded in next to the piano, plus the practice cello Herr Müller let Giselle use so she wouldn't have to haul her own cello around on the train. Instead, there was a round table with four chairs set for an afternoon tea. The walls were lined with old books; the window was open exactly one inch.

I set down my violin and looked at the girls. They shrugged. I guessed they hadn't gotten the memo about the tea party, either.

"Are we celebrating something?" I asked. There was a vase with tulips in the middle of the table.

"You ladies have been working so very hard," Herr Müller said. "Just this one time I will make for you a treat." He motioned us to sit and poured us all cups of tea.

Herr Müller was bald as an egg. Apparently his hair had all migrated down to form one massive gray eyebrow. I'd never heard him say how old he was, but based on the number of orchestras he had played in or composed for, I'd have guessed he was one hundred and twenty-three. He looked out the window and didn't take the first sip of tea or even pass around the cake. I waited for him to start, but he looked completely lost in thought. I lifted the cake plate and held it so Vivi could serve herself a slice.

"Ladies, you are technically fine players, each one of you," Herr Müller said, turning back toward us. "I am very proud of your musical progress."

Giselle and I traded a look, and Vivian hid a smile behind her long sweep of blond hair. What had gotten into him? It wasn't like Herr Müller to be all mushy. I kept my mouth shut except for *Danke* and *Bitte*. I passed the treats, wondering if tea before international music competitions was one of those customs we hadn't studied yet in our German language and culture class at school.

"Yes," Herr Müller went on. "You play with skill and also the warmth of good friendship. The best music comes from the heart in this way."

Now I was getting worried. Herr Müller was all about technique and precision. He ended every single piece we had

ever played with a list of things in need of "development."
Herr Müller stood up and walked to the window. He surveyed the window box with its required planting of red
geraniums.

"You have made such progress. I am very proud."

"Is there something on your mind?" Vivian asked. "You
don't sound like yourself today."

"I am not myself," Herr Müller said. "Not myself at all.
I'm sorry, I will not be taking you to the Solo and Ensemble
Contest this weekend. We will have to cancel our journey to
Paris."

"What?"

"Why?"

"Aren't we playing well enough?"

"No, it is not you. I need to have surgery. Not to worry. It
is only a small operation. Unfortunately, it cannot wait. I am
so sorry. I will be in the hospital for the next five days."

"Oh." I slumped back in my chair. I'd packed for the trip
last week. I'd saved every dime from babysitting the neigh-
bor kids. I'd told my aunt Cassandra from Minnesota that I
was going. She had sent me a camera for my birthday so I'd
have one in Paris.

Vivian asked Herr Müller the kind of polite questions
grown-ups ask about being sick. I didn't even hear his
answers.

So this is it, I thought. We'll never play together again.
Our parents had decided to let us go with only Herr Müller

for a chaperone because they had known him for years, but mostly I think they let us do it because they were all so busy, and they hated taking time off work.

At the end of tea, Herr Müller gave us a note to our parents about canceling the contest, letters of reference for our new music teachers, and a big bar of chocolate for each of us. It was the kind we all hated, with the raisins and hazelnuts in it. We walked out to the street, blinking more from shock than from the late-afternoon sunshine.

We shuffled down the street hardly noticing it was a beautiful day. After a dreary, dark winter and an equally dreary, damp spring, it was the warmest day of the year so far. I felt numb. The trip to Paris was the thing I was using to keep from thinking about saying goodbye to Giselle and Vivian when we moved in less than a month—one last trip for just the three of us. Berlin was the longest I'd been stationed anywhere in my whole life. I'd been in the same school for three years. When we drove somewhere on the weekend, some of the streets actually looked familiar. I even had a favorite restaurant down by the lake. We'd gone there to play at the beach and eat dinner two birthdays in a row. And I'd known Giselle and Vivian longer than I'd known anyone except my own brothers.

Vivian trudged along kicking at gravel. "There has to be a way to still go," she said. "Can't your parents take us?"

Giselle shook her head. "My dad is hosting that military ball, remember? The last one for American forces stationed in Berlin. It's such a big deal! That really old chancellor who got the Peace Prize is going to come, and some famous writer, plus officers from the French and British and German armies. Mom has been sweating the details for months. Do you know how many kinds of protocol there are for all those people? Scary."

"Oh yeah," Vivi said, "Mom and Dad are going, too. And Mom's got some other big diplomatic thing this weekend. Something about what to do about all these little countries that are wanting to leave the Soviet Union. It's crazy. She's on the phone constantly. She even got this weird new kind of phone that you can carry around in your briefcase."

They both looked at me.

"Look, Giselle, if your dad's working, mine is." My dad was on General Johnson's staff. "And my mom has been working a ton of extra shifts at the hospital." I shrugged. "Sorry."

"We aren't going to give up, are we?" Giselle said. "Come on! We have to think of something!"

Which is what I imagine officers say when they want their enlisted men to solve whatever the problem is. I started lining up excuses in my head. It's not like Mom wanted to work the hours of a crazy person, but without her income, we could never afford a good violin and lessons.

"We need gelato!" Giselle commanded. "We can't possibly think clearly without ice cream."

"Exactly," Vivian said, turning right instead of left at the corner. There was a new shop on the other side of the Brandenburg Gate. "If everyone had just sat down for gelato together every afternoon, the Cold War would have been over a decade ago."

Giselle laughed. "Ice cream—the instrument of world peace! Why else would we have kept Italy around all this time?"

Vivaldi and the *Four Seasons,* I thought. Rossini, Puccini, and the best violin makers in the entire world! But I didn't say anything.

We turned north away from the S-Bahn and toward the Reichstag and the center of Berlin. It was hard to believe that only seven months ago this street had run beside the Berlin Wall—a concrete slab twenty feet tall, behind it a no-man's-land with barbed wire, land mines, and armed guards ready to gun down anyone who tried to cross. Now we could just stroll right through the Brandenburg Gate into East Berlin.

Vivian walked in front, and even though I'd gone into East Berlin once already with my family, Giselle and I hesitated on the western side of the Brandenburg Gate. When your dad was a soldier stationed in Cold War Germany, it wasn't just a wall to keep Communists from running away from home. It was a barrier between us and the enemy. Except they weren't the enemy anymore. They were nothing but sad, shabby former Communists in a broken-down city that used to be the glamour capital of Europe: richer than London and wilder than Paris. Giselle looked at me, and I shrugged back, and we both laughed to cover our pause and crossed over into enemy territory.

The area right around the Brandenburg Gate had been cleaned and tidied, for the sake of TV cameras, mostly. Last winter it had seemed like every news station on the planet was covering the New Year's Eve dance-on-top-of-the-wall party. But the crowds were gone now. Powder gray crumbs of concrete crunched underfoot as we crossed where the Wall had been. Off to the right was a crew of German Army Pioneers testing for land mines. To the left a long line of dump trucks stood waiting for work crews to fill them with concrete and steel.

The East German neighborhood beyond the Brandenburg Gate was full of shuttered buildings and the empty doorways of apartments that belonged to people who had left everything behind for a chance to live in the West. The main signs of life were the street peddlers with their wooden trays full of Communist souvenirs, mostly Soviet army gadgets— insignia, watches, pocketknives, and the like. They were all young, clean-shaven men with cigarettes and tattooed arms.

"You buy, miss?" one of them said as I looked over his tray of army badges. Some of the insignia were easy to figure out—parachutes and submarines look the same no matter whose side you're on—but others were harder to guess. I wanted the rank insignia that was the Soviet version of sergeant major for my dad. Father's Day was less than a month away. Dad had a whole collection of army coins and patches from his twenty years in the service. Giselle glanced at the pins and patches and then glared at the vendor.

"It's not legal to sell these things, is it?"

Giselle's dad was the commanding general of American forces in Berlin. You'd think she had rank herself, the way she bossed people around, even grown-ups. The crazy thing was, most people did what she told them to just because of the way she said things. Or maybe she could pull it off because she was going to be six feet tall, possibly by next week.

"No, miss, is very proper." The peddler held up both hands to show he wasn't hiding anything.

"Oh yeah? Explain that." Giselle pointed to an open sack on the ground. It held what looked like tiny black pineapples.

"Oh my gosh!" I said. "Are those hand grenades?" I took a step closer.

"Jody!" Giselle shouted. "Don't move!"

I froze.

"Those fat Frisbee things in the box behind the grenades. I'm pretty sure those are land mines."

I slowly edged back toward her and Vivian, clutching my violin case across my chest.

"What do you people think you are doing?" Giselle said, putting on her father's command voice. "You can't have ordnance around civilians. It's dangerous. You fools do know that that stuff tends to blow up from time to time?" She stretched up to her full five feet ten, hands on hips and glaring at the peddlers like they were a pack of bratty third graders.

They started to look nervous. A few of them glanced down the street like they were expecting Giselle to call up her own reinforcements.

"You stay right here, now. I'm going over to that phone booth to call the Polizei." She turned away, shaking her head. "Land mines! Idiots!"

The peddlers shoved their wares into sacks and dashed off to the graffiti-tagged back alleys of East Berlin.

Giselle surveyed their departure with satisfaction. I just shook my head, once again dazzled by Giselle's flair for command. It must be genetic.

"Think we should tell our dads?"

"Maybe," Giselle said. "If he actually comes home tonight. I need to catch mine in the right mood for talking."

I totally got what she was talking about. Dad had worked all night last night, too. I'd heard him come in for a shower and a shave about five a.m. Mom had gotten up to fix him breakfast and have their usual argument about the hours he worked, and Dad had had his usual pot of deeply dark coffee and then gone straight back to work without a nap.

"He probably knows," Giselle said. She looked down the side street. "Dad talks to the German police commissioner about Soviet soldiers a lot these days."

I nodded and kept walking. Without the peddlers, the street was practically empty. There had been stuff in the news about the Russian soldiers not getting paid. I wasn't a genius history student or anything, but it seemed like if you were going to stop paying soldiers, it would be smart to take away their weapons first.

We walked to the corner where Gelato Mario was an oasis of red tables and sparkling clean windows in a drab gray block of empty storefronts. I held open the door, and we filed in, dropping our cases and backpacks in the booth by the window.

From behind the ice cream counter Mario flashed a movie-star smile. "*Buon giorno!* What will it be, ladies?"

Vivian smiled. She said something in flawless Italian. Vivian was no one special; her mom was just the U.S. consul general to West Berlin, and Vivian was one of the ten smartest kids on the planet. She came to eighth grade for half days. The rest of the time she studied math and languages at the high school, and dance at the Berlin Opera Ballet. I could barely keep up with square dancing in PE. If I took ballet with dancers who spoke German and a teacher who spoke French and an accompanist who spoke Russian, my head would explode.

I studied the ice cream choices: hazelnut, espresso, cherry, spumoni.

"What? No mint chip?" I said. "What's the matter? Is it against the law to have mint chip in this country?"

"It is not wise," Mario replied in the grave tone most grown-ups reserved for talking about the economy. "With chocolate you must have orange or amaretto. Chocolate mint is not correct."

"Let's have sundaes," Giselle butted in. "I'll treat."

"Mmm, yes," Vivian said. "Let's have doubles."

They weren't actually sundaes in the whipped cream, nuts, and hot fudge way. In Germany they made sundaes with liquor and fruit. Apparently it was perfectly legal to sell alcohol to kids, so long as ice cream was involved. I used to hate it when we first moved here, but now I'm not sure I want to go back to plain old banana splits.

"I don't know, guys," I said. "If I come home smelling like rum and cherries, Mom's going to think we skipped out on our music lesson."

"So we won't go home," Giselle said. "Not right away. We can tell our moms we went to the National Gallery. They aren't going to mind if we look at art, are they?"

I should have said no. I should have gone straight home on the train like the good girl I'd always been and not made my parents worry, but it was our last afternoon together, and I didn't want it to end.

Unter den Linden, East Berlin

We took our paper cups of gelato to the window booth and watched the peddlers drift back onto the main street to attract the early commuters. Except for the part about them selling weapons, they looked quite picturesque with their old-fashioned wooden trays and boxes, standing under the bright yellow flowers of the linden trees. There weren't many takers for their wares. East Berliners had no money and no interest in Russian souvenirs, and West Berliners had gotten over their initial curiosity about the East and never crossed.

East Berlin was like a giant ghost town where the ghosts weren't quite dead yet. The East Berliners putted around in smelly cars and sat in clumps on park benches. Nobody seemed to have a job. Trainloads of East Germans had come over the border, crowding into refugee centers and moving in with relatives they hadn't seen in forty years. There were a few gamblers like Mario who had come over from the West with cash and a business idea, but most West Berliners looked at the run-down filth of the East and asked themselves why they'd wanted reunification in the first place.

"What a mess," Vivian said, waving her spoon in the direction of a trash-filled doorway across the street.

"Isn't there anywhere pretty on this side of town?" I said. "I can't believe these are the same Germans. Back on the West side they practically vacuum the parks."

"I've heard it's pretty by the river," Giselle said. "Not as pretty as Paris, but let's find a nice spot, and we can at least pretend it's the Seine."

We grabbed our stuff and headed outside. It was hot on the pavement, and the wind was absolutely still, which was rare for Berlin and definitely a preview of coming attractions when we moved to Texas at the end of June.

We'd lived in Texas when I was five. I remembered two things about Fort Hood. The First Cavalry had real horses. Mom used to take me out to the stables where I could watch the cavalry horses, and sometimes one would come over and take a carrot from my hand. I'd loved those horses. I also remembered the day I got distracted petting one of them and stepped in a fire ant hill. Hundreds of red ants swarmed up my legs and bit me so many times, I had to go to the hospital. I missed three whole days of school. I cried because I missed my kindergarten teacher so much. She was pretty and cheerful, and she called me Sunshine even though I didn't have blond hair. She taught us to read by singing, and she let me strum her guitar. We moved to Fort Drum in New York two months later. After that I learned not to love my teachers so much. Berlin was my fourth school in seven years.

Like she was reading my mind, Giselle said, "So has your dad decided where to retire?"

I shrugged. "He's got interviews set up in Houston and Dallas and San Antonio. He's not even looking outside Texas."

"What does your mom say?"

"There'll be a hospital no matter where we go. Emergency rooms always need nurses, so she's not worried about a job the way my dad is."

"I don't think he needs to worry," Giselle said. "Dad's going to give him a great letter. He likes Sergeant Major Field. 'Hardest-working sergeant major I ever had,' he says. 'You never hear him complain.'"

Not where General Johnson can hear it, I thought.

I turned to Vivian. "What about you? Where will you go for high school now that the school on base is closing?"

"They're going to send me to boarding school."

"Cool!" Giselle said, turning us left into a park along the bank of the Spree River.

"In Switzerland," Vivian added.

"Hey," I said, "I went to Garmisch on vacation last winter. That's practically Switzerland. It was really pretty."

"Do you have any idea how rich those girls are going to be? Mom was going on about how the duchess of this and the heir to that will be attending, like this is going to make me feel like I fit in."

I didn't know what to say about that. Vivian always seemed rich to me.

"Well, at least everybody who comes to your school will be new," Giselle said. "Dad's looking for a house in Palo Alto, next to the university where he's going to teach. It's this really old neighborhood and everybody has lived there forever. I bet I'm the only new girl at school."

"Well, at least they aren't expecting you to have a title and a thousand dollars a month in spending money."

"At least at the boarding school there will be other girls who are looking for a friend and clubs you are allowed to join," Giselle said. "I don't know what those girls wear or what music they think is good or what sports they think are cool." She picked up a broken paving stone from the path and chucked it clear across the grass and into the river. "What if those Palo Alto girls don't play sports? If this turns out to be one of those cheerleader-only towns, I'm going to kill myself!"

She picked up a bigger stone and threw it into the river. It almost made it to the other side. When Giselle pitched on our school softball team, she made the batters cry.

"It's not exactly a picnic to have everyone expect you to dress like a fashion model every day," Vivian said, kicking a stone down the path. "As soon as they find out I got in on academic merit, they are going to start bugging me to let them copy my homework."

Giselle gave her a withering look. "It's better than cheerleading–trust me!"

Vivian opened her mouth to say something back, but then she turned away, swinging her hair forward to make a don't-talk-to-me curtain around her face. Giselle muttered some cuss words and in a dozen long strides was yards ahead of us.

It was green and quiet by the river, and there were pink flowers on the trees. We walked along without talking for a while, and then Vivian motioned for me to go talk to Giselle, because fixing things up between them was my main job in the group–that and second violin.

"If the kids in your new neighborhood are mean to you, you could run away," I called ahead to Giselle. She slowed down but didn't turn around. "You could run away to Paris and live in a tiny but totally hip apartment and play your cello on the street corners."

"That would be perfect!" Vivian chimed in. She was dying to go to Paris and live a romantically impoverished artist's life. "And then a handsome French painter will start painting your picture and fall in love with you, and–"

"Don't fall in love," I said. "Everyone falls in love in Paris." I turned around to glare at Vivian, and Giselle laughed.

"Yeah," Giselle said. "Besides, you should never fall in love with an artist. Have you ever looked at their photos at the museum? Not one of those boys knows how to dress, and they don't look like they take baths, either."

"Exactly," I said. "You should play on your street corner every day—sad, dramatic, romantic songs that you compose on the spot, and some famous old maestro will fall in love with your music and make you his protégée."

"Right," Vivian added, "and then Jody and I will move to Paris, and I'll go to art school and draw all your album covers, and Jody will ... What are you going to do in Paris?"

First violin for a change, I thought. No, better! Concertmaster! Famous composer! Right, me with the secondhand sweaters and home haircuts. I'm not the type to attract fame. I kept that thought to myself because Vivian and Giselle were really into my story, and thinking about Paris was way better than thinking about trying to find new friends in a new town.

"I'll be your manager," I said. "Someone has to look out for you, because that maestro is going to turn out to be a snake. He'll try to control your career and crush your art."

"Crush my art?" Giselle let in some of her father's North Carolina accent. "Bring it on! I'll crush that maestro like a bug."

She probably could, too. Giselle took fencing three times a week. She had a girly figure, but I bet she could bench-press a pickup truck. She was going to scare the heck out of those California girls. We caught up to her and walked side by side.

"So I'll make you ditch the maestro, and we'll start up an all-girl orchestra, the best one in Paris, maybe in all of Europe." I paused a minute to make sure Giselle and Vivian were really done being mad. "What do you think?"

Vivi sighed. "I just want to go to a normal American school and do the things other kids get to do and I only get to read about. Mom thinks I'm having this great international experience, but changing schools constantly is exactly the same horrible thing every time, no matter what country you're in."

We came to a railroad bridge with an inviting stretch of shade underneath. I set my violin down in the shade and kicked off my shoes. Giselle did, too, but Vivian held back.

"I wouldn't wade in there. I hear it's horribly polluted."

Giselle took a dramatic sniff. I could smell machine oil and something worse: vinegar, maybe, or battery acid. There was a yellow sheen on top of the water.

"Eww, Jody, let's go sit up there." Vivian pointed to the top of the riverbank, right under the railroad tracks. She took one of the icky green army towels that everyone used for PE out of her backpack, and I followed her up the slope. We dropped our stuff, spread out the towel, and sat down. A blackberry patch grew on one side of the train tracks and a clump of evergreens on the other, hiding us from view. Giselle dug in her backpack for the cassette player and speakers so we could all hear.

"I don't see why you're so worried about those rich girls, Vivi," I said quietly. "I like you. And I've never made you do my homework, not even once." I tried to look sympathetic, but sometimes these two seemed so far out of my league, I couldn't believe they even talked to me.

I was about to change the subject when we heard the sputter of an army jeep on the road above us. Brakes squealed. Men jumped out. Giselle shot me a look and we both froze, because even when they were losing, those guys were enemies. I turned to Vivian and held up a finger to quiet her, but Giselle went ahead and clamped a hand over her mouth. Vivi tended to scream, even when it was only a spider.

We looked up and saw two men in uniform dragging a third man along the narrow iron grating that ran beside the train tracks. They were shouting to each other in a way that made me sure they were angry even though they weren't speaking English or German. I turned to Vivian as Giselle let her go. Vivi knew lots of languages. Her eyes were wide with shock. She inched back into the shadows under the bridge, tugging at my sleeve to follow her.

There was a shrill whistle from a freight train a ways up the track. The man who was being dragged began to struggle.

"Nyet!" he groaned. He twisted and tried to tug his arms free. *"Nyet!"*

One of the soldiers hit the man over the head. He crumpled to the bed of the railroad tracks. There was more shouting. Vivian gasped and Giselle clamped a hand over her mouth again. I inched to the edge of our hiding place to get a better look. The shape of the fallen man's body made a silhouette on the walkway. The other men bent over to pick him up. There was a red star in a gold circle on the cap of one and a red-edged shoulder board on the other.

Russian officers!

The tracks hummed. The train whistle sounded again, much closer. The officers dragged the man upright. The train came around the final bend and roared over our heads. We curled up, hiding our faces on our knees to protect ourselves from the gravel and sparks that rained down on us. I squeezed my eyes shut against the blowing dust. Just as the last car passed overhead, I heard a splash.

I jumped to my feet and strained to look for a body in the water without leaving the shadows. There was nothing, not even a ring in the water to show where the man had fallen. My heart hammered in my throat three times and then five and then ten as I scanned the width of the river. The body bobbed to the surface, bumped against a bridge abutment, and began to float under the bridge, facedown in the oily water.

3

Under the Railroad Bridge, East Berlin

The officers retreated across the bridge and climbed into their jeep. The engine sputtered to life, and they sped off in the direction of the Soviet army barracks.

"Come on!" I scrambled down the slope to the edge of the river, not even noticing the rocks under my bare feet. The current slowly turned the body as it passed under the bridge.

"Oh my God! Oh my God! They killed him!" Giselle said. She ran behind me.

"We can't just leave him in there. Help me," I yelled. I scanned the river's edge for a good spot to wade out. The body bumped against the downstream abutment, and the slow current held it there. "Hold on!" I reached for Giselle, and we locked hands. I peered into the water, looking for solid footing, but in the shadow of the bridge there was nothing to see.

"Here goes!" I inched forward on the rocky river bottom.

Giselle clasped Vivian's hand and followed me. The

water was biting cold but not fast enough to knock me over. I gasped as it soaked my jeans. My hands shook. Giselle leaned out with her long arms, and Vivian kept her feet on solid ground. Only a few more steps, and I'd be able to grab the soldier's boot.

"Come on, Giselle, just a little farther!"

"He's too far."

"No, I'm almost there." I leaned out farther and took a step. "Almost there." I gritted my teeth to keep them from chattering as the water line rose to my ribs. I leaned harder, trusting my whole weight to Giselle's grip, and snagged the boot.

"Pull!" I yelled. Giselle grunted and tugged me toward her. I dragged the body away from the piling. It came easily, like the blow-up alligator I pulled around the swimming pool with my little brothers on it. I pulled the body by the heel, shivering so hard I almost lost my grip. We stumbled toward shore. When we reached the edge, Vivian took hold of the soldier's feet, and Giselle and I grabbed the back of his shirt to haul him out of the water. At first he was easy to lift, but as soon as he was out of the water, it felt like the body gained two hundred pounds. He was limp and cold. We finally dragged him free of the water and stretched him out facedown on the gravel of the riverbank.

"Oh my God," Vivi said as we backed away. "They killed him."

"Now what do we do?" Giselle said.

I shook the water off my arms and squeezed out the bottom edge of my T-shirt. There was a dark orange ring of scum around my ribs, and my wet jeans stuck to my legs.

"Should we roll him over?" Giselle said.

I nodded, still catching my breath. Giselle and Vivi grabbed a sleeve and a pant leg to turn the body over. He was young, and he had jet-black hair that was longer than most American soldiers wear it. His face was bruised and swollen. There was a scar under his lower lip, and the top one was split and bleeding.

"Who would do this?" I said, swallowing back nausea. "Why beat him up if you were only going to kill him anyway?"

The girls edged away, but I couldn't resist touching his hand. The second I did, his head flopped to the side and his mouth fell open. Scummy brown water rolled out. Vivian screamed, and Giselle staggered backward a few steps.

"Oh my God, Jody," Vivian said. "He's not dead!"

Instinct kicked in. I knelt by his head and checked for breathing. I tilted his chin back and gave three puffs of air. His chest rose up and down just like the plastic dummy in Mom's CPR class. I leaned over him and gave three compressions in the middle of his chest. They made a hideous sucking sound. I gave another rescue breath. I could taste oil and bleach from the river, but his chest went up and down just like it should.

Vivian sat on the bank a little above me, hugged her knees

to her chest, and stared at the drowned man, but Giselle came and knelt shoulder to shoulder with me.

"Sorry I freaked, Jody. Show me what to do."

I put her hands on the right spot. "Down, up, down, up. Nice and steady." I scooted up by his head and waited for five compressions before giving another puff of air.

"Vivi, don't just sit there!" I ordered. "Get help!"

Vivian sat. She looked from the bridge to the body to the road, where the soldiers had driven away. Her mouth moved, but she didn't make a sound.

"I mean it! Go!"

And then the body moved. It squeezed from the middle like it was trying to curl up in a ball. It jerked again and took in a breath.

"We have to roll him onto his side, Giselle. Come on—you move his hips and I'll do the shoulders. Ready? One, two, three."

We both heaved. The second we had him on his side, he barfed out a stream of yellowish water. We jumped out of the way. He threw up again and again and made the most inhuman moaning noise. Vivian came up behind us and put an arm around each of us. We stood frozen while the drowned man fought river water out of his stomach.

My parents had talked about death, plenty of times. Mom's an emergency-room nurse, and Dad's a career soldier. But here it was, right in front of me. That soldier was dead, or almost dead, when I pulled him out of the river. He was limp and cold, and now he was a real person, writhing in pain but alive.

I had no idea what to do next. The CPR class never said what to do when a person got better. It was always "Call an ambulance and help will be there in a few minutes."

"We have to get him to a hospital," Giselle said. "Where's the nearest phone booth?"

"Wait," Vivian said. "We have to think about this. He's a Russian, right?"

"And the men who tried to kill him were officers," I added.

Vivian paced along the water's edge. "We can't take him to the hospital, Giselle, they'll give him back."

"What are you talking about?" Giselle turned toward Vivian, glaring. "We have to help him."

"He's a soldier. He belongs to his unit. They'll send him straight back to those guys who beat him up."

"How can they do that?" I said. "It's just wrong. Can't they arrest the guys who tried to murder him?"

"I don't think the Germans get to say what happens when one Russian tries to kill another one. Besides, I think technically he's a deserter."

"What?" Giselle yelled. "Technically they heaved him off a bridge!"

"Yeah, but they're not going to admit it, are they?" Vivian said. "They'll say it was a training accident or an attempted suicide. They have a terrible safety record."

Giselle nodded. I'd heard the same thing.

"Isn't there some kind of sanctuary or immunity or something?" I asked. "Look at him. They tortured him."

"They are horribly mean to their own soldiers," Giselle said. "Dad says they use physical punishment all the time."

The man groaned and lifted his head an inch. *"Vodah,"* he said.

"What? What did he say?" Giselle and I both looked at Vivian for a translation.

"He wants water," Vivian said.

"Water?" I said. "Do they even have drinking fountains in East Berlin? Bet they don't work."

"He can have my juice box," Vivian said. "I saved it from lunch. He can have my sandwich, too." Vivian had been on a different diet every month since fifth grade. I hadn't seen her eat anything but Jell-O, Skittles, and bananas all week. She went back up to where we had been sitting and rooted around in her backpack.

Giselle circled the soldier, looking him over carefully. "I don't think he's armed," she said. "And even if he did have a sidearm, it wouldn't work when it's wet."

The soldier sat up a little further and then slumped forward, exhausted from that little effort. He looked up and down the riverbank and then at the road behind him. He spat river water onto the ground and turned toward Giselle and me.

"Hey," I said, wondering what you were supposed to say

to a non-English-speaking almost-dead guy. We got German language class at school, but it didn't exactly cover this. "Umm, *wie geht's?* How are you?"

"I live," he replied very slowly.

"You speak English?" I took a step closer.

"Yes." He tapped a colored patch on his sleeve. "Translator."

Vivian bounded up with her school lunch. She said something that sounded Russian, poked the plastic straw into the corner of the juice box, and handed it to the soldier. The box looked ridiculously small in his hand, and he glanced at it from several angles before lifting it in a little toast.

"Zum wohl." It was the German toast we all learned at school—"to your good health." He drained the juice in one long swallow.

"You aren't *wohl,* though," I said, squeezing water out of my jeans as I spoke. "You aren't even a little bit *wohl.* Look at you." I pointed to the cuts on his face. His right foot pointed off at a weird angle.

"Yes." He nodded in the direction of his leg. "Broken." He ran a finger along his ribs on the left side. "Very much, probably, broken."

"We have to get him to a hospital," Giselle said. "Look, he's shivering."

"No! *Nyet!*" The Russian dropped the juice box in the dirt and tried to drag his body away from us. "Please!"

"But your leg is broken," Giselle went on, switching to command volume. "You can't just stay here."

"No hospital, please! You save me!"

"What?" Giselle snapped back.

"Hospital will send me back. They start killing me all over again. You save me."

"See?" Vivian said, glaring at Giselle for a change.

"But why are your own officers hurting you?" Giselle demanded. "Officers aren't like that."

"They hate me because I am not Russian. Because I will not do an evil thing like a man with no soul." He looked straight into my eyes as he said it, and even though his were streaked with blood, he seemed much too young to be a soldier.

"I only want to go home. Home to my own country." He kept looking at me, and I had to make myself look away.

"What are you talking about?" I said. "Isn't this your country? It's probably the hypothermia making you talk like a crazy person. Look." I turned to my friends. "We have to get him dry, at least, or he'll die all over again."

"I've got my skunky PE towel and gym clothes," Giselle offered. "He can just have them. We've got plenty more at home."

"Can you get out of your wet clothes?" I asked him.

"*Da*. Is only pain. I can do it." He looked over his shoulder again and back up to the bridge.

"They're gone," I told him. "We'll hide you if they come back."

"Thank you." He bowed his head to me.

Giselle dug her PE clothes and towel out of her backpack. She and Vivian went down by the river, but I stayed and stared at the soldier. His face was so beat up. Maybe I was trying to guess what he looked like when he hadn't just been murdered. He unbuttoned his uniform jacket and let it drop in the dirt. Apparently T-shirts the color of dog poop are a military universal, because this guy had one just like all of Dad's. He tugged it over his head, groaning as he did. I saw that he was as fair-skinned as me. He had more muscles than any boy in my class, but he moved like an old man, and it was easy to see why. There was a ring of bruises around the bottom of his ribs, one in the shape of the sole of a boot. There were three long red marks over his shoulders like he'd been beaten with a stick.

How could people do this? I wished I had some magic remedy to make all that pain go away. He tugged on Giselle's PE shirt, which was skintight on him, but he left the shorts on the ground and wrapped the towel around his waist, squeezing water out of his pants.

I hopped up to get him another gym towel from my backpack. I could hear Giselle and Vivian arguing about what to do with the soldier. Vivian was so smart; she was usually the problem solver of the group. You could ask her anything: the capital of Yugoslavia, what money is called in Czechoslovakia, how to order a hamburger in French. It wasn't normal. But this time she didn't have answers.

I kept imagining those Russian officers. What could possibly make them try to kill their own man? Soldiers fight sometimes. I guess that's true in every army. There were rumors last fall about a soldier at our barracks who hit his girlfriend. Some of the other enlisted men saw it. That night when he got back to the barracks, a bunch of them beat him up so he'd get the picture about not hitting women. What if those officers beat him up because he was bad to his girlfriend or because he was a thief? I got a shiver, and not because I was sitting around in wet jeans. Suddenly I didn't want to be near him. I got up and ran down to Vivi and Giselle by the river.

"I don't know," Giselle was saying. "Why should we trust him? He's a Communist, and apparently even other Communists hate him."

"We should take him back to the army base," Vivian said. "There will be a hospital there at least."

"And in what wheelbarrow are we going to take him home?" Giselle said. "He can't walk; we can't carry him."

"We can't just leave him here. He's hurt," I said. "If we walk away and let him die, we're no better than those Communists."

"Maybe we can leave him here," Giselle said. "Look at him."

We turned to see the soldier sitting up with his uniform in a heap beside him. We went closer. His lips weren't so purple as before, and he wasn't shivering.

"Are you going to be okay?" I said. "Maybe we should call the Polizei?"

"No! Please. No Polizei. They send me straight back to my unit. No. They spit on me first, and then they send me back."

"Why?"

"Is a bitter history between the Germans and the Soviets."

"Well, there isn't exactly a great history between America and Germany, either, but we get along fine now."

The soldier looked out over the river as he spoke. "Nazis killed twenty million Russians in the war, and when we finally fought them out of our homelands and back here to this city—well, Soviet soldiers took their revenge on the women and children of Berlin. It was cruel, and it was long ago. People do not forget."

"But none of that is your fault. That was long before you were even born. Won't the Polizei help you?"

He shook his head. "A soldier belongs to his army. Is settled law. Anyone you tell about me will send me back." He turned to stare up at me, and I've never seen a person look more exhausted. "Please—let me live. Let me hide. Let me rest."

"I bet he could hide here," Vivian said. "In the whole time we've been down here, we haven't seen or heard a soul. It's kind of creepy."

"Is empty here in East Berlin," the soldier said. "All people running to the West."

"Are you going to be okay?" I asked.

"We can come back tomorrow after school and bring food," Vivian said. "And in the meantime he can have this." She took Herr Müller's chocolate bar out of her purse and set it on the ground.

"Good idea." I said. Giselle and I added our chocolate bars.

The soldier looked at our stack of Ritter Sports and put his hand over his heart as if we had given him something unspeakably precious.

"Let's move him there," Giselle said, pointing to our hiding place under the bridge. "He'll be harder to see."

Giselle lifted from under the soldier's arms, and Vivi took the good leg and started to tug.

"I'm going to go over there and put on my PE clothes," I said, waving in the general direction of some shrubs.

The other two half dragged the soldier up the bank to a sheltered spot. He tried his best to help with his good leg, but mostly he spent his energy trying not to scream in pain. They settled him under the bushes and put his wet uniform out of sight behind him. Giselle made a pillow of her fencing-team jacket. The soldier leaned back on the pillow, breathing as hard as if he'd run a mile. He waved us away.

"You go. I sleep."

"We'll come check on you tomorrow," I said.

We gathered up our backpacks and violins and headed down the river toward the main road and the gelato shop. The sun felt good on my bare arms and legs, but even so, I was shivering from the memory of dark water and the way the river felt like it was pulling me in.

"We never do stuff together on days we don't have a lesson," I said. "How are we going to get permission to come back into downtown Berlin?"

"We just need to figure out a reason to get together," Giselle said. "We can say we're at the library or something. Mom likes it when I go to the library."

"Here's an unprecedented idea," Vivian said. "We're a trio; we could get together and say we're practicing."

"But we never practice together," I said.

"Well, my mom is always bugging me to bring you guys over to play," Vivi said. "I'll just say I'm doing it at Giselle's house and Giselle can say she's at your house."

I had never bothered to invite them to my place. No way would my neighbors want to see the general's daughter hanging around enlisted housing.

"Yeah, that would work great," I said, "except our moms call each other."

Giselle actually slumped a little bit, and we all walked slower as we turned onto Unter den Linden, with the Brandenburg Gate at the far end leading us back to West Berlin. The shadows from the trees on either side of the street stretched eastward, and even the uncollected garbage from side streets couldn't drown out the sweet smell of those tiny yellow linden flowers.

Once we crossed into West Berlin, there were plenty of people around. The S-Bahn stop at the Potsdamer Platz was packed with commuters, so we had to find separate seats. Usually when I had a few moments to myself on the train, I took out my music notebook and worked on my songs. Last year I decided to write a canon for us that made all the instruments in the trio equal players. I finished the violin parts last summer, but the cello part was much harder. It took me months, and even though I'd finished the "Canon for Three Friends" in March, I still wasn't satisfied. It was kind of simple compared to the rest of the music we played, and I was too shy to ask the girls to play it.

But today, I kept working over the matter of how to get back into East Berlin to help our soldier. I racked my brain to think of what normal girls did together after school. Movies? There was only one theater on the army base, and our folks would hear about it if we didn't show up. Bowling? My folks or people who knew them would be there. The officers' club? I wasn't even allowed in the door.

I got to thinking about it, and even though Giselle and Vivian were the best friends I'd ever had, all we did was eat lunch together at school, travel to music competitions once a year, and take the train to Herr Müller's. Once, we stopped at the Christmas market on the way home from lessons to get crystal ornaments for our moms. But we never just got together for no reason like other girls did. I felt so close to them when we played a piece of music, especially a hard one we had really worked on. But they were strangers to me, too. And I wondered for the hundredth time what it was going to be like to choose a hometown and buy a house and live in one place forever. I wondered what kids were like who had never traveled.

Dad hated it when I moped about army life. "We have good memories in a thousand places," he'd say. "You can find your way in any size city or town. You can make a home for yourself anywhere, and that makes you a thousand times richer than those hometown Hannahs who've never gone a mile on their own."

He was right about getting around. My cousins in Chicago weren't allowed to ride their own commuter train, even though the whole system was in English. I'd been riding the Berlin trains alone since I was ten, and Mom didn't even check up on me to see if I'd made it to my music lesson.

That's it! I stood up and tapped Giselle on the shoulder. Vivian's stop was coming up. "I've got an idea!" I said. "Get off here and we'll talk."

Giselle grabbed her backpack and followed Vivian and me out onto the platform. The train door hissed shut behind us, and the train rumbled off to the south. I motioned them over to a bench.

"We can say we're going to Herr Müller's," I said. "To practice for the competition. It's perfect! Our parents want us to win, and they hate to talk to Herr Müller on the phone because of his accent."

There was a moment of silence while the girls digested my plan.

"Plus they don't know Herr Müller's canceled yet, because he's telling them in the letters he gave us," I said, tapping the folder where I kept my sheet music.

"And if we don't give them the letter, they'll still think we're going," Vivi added. "And it gives us a reason not just to get together, but to head back down in the direction of our wounded soldier's bridge. Jody, you are a genius! Mom doesn't care where I go, so long as I'm with people she knows."

"Ditto," Giselle said. "Oh my gosh, this could really work. You two could leave your violins at home and fill your cases with clothes and other stuff our soldier needs."

"Look," I said, "I can only bring food. Kyle and Tyler eat constantly, so Mom will never miss a jar of peanut butter, but no way am I stealing Dad's clothes."

"No problem, I'll get the clothes," Giselle said. "My dad's bigger than him, but better too big than too small."

"I'll see what I can find out about foreign soldiers and if they have any protection from their own army," Vivian said. "There are lots of law books in Mom's study, and her secretary helps me with my homework all the time."

That would explain why her papers were always perfectly

typed and mine were full of cross-outs and my brothers'
jammy fingerprints.

"Great. So we'll meet after school tomorrow," I said.

Giselle and I hopped back on the train to Zehlendorf. It
was even more crowded than before, so we stood without
talking, but my head was buzzing with plans the whole
way home.

U.S. Army Base, Zehlendorf, West Berlin

i walked the dozen blocks from the train stop to the enlisted apartment buildings. Usually I stopped at the PX for my favorite candy bar, but that day I went straight home. I strolled past the familiar places on base: the army hospital, the post office, the day care, and then the motor pool. All the HAZMAT trucks were lined up by the gate with their engines running, and a bunch of guys stood around in those horribly hot-looking rubber suits. Seems like they could have picked a less sunny day for a chemical weapons drill.

There was no way I'd be able to sneak anything out of the house with Dad around. Dad was all about the routine and kids having responsibilities, even my little brothers. He monitored my homework, my chores, my music practice, and my phone calls. If Mom didn't stand up to him every once in a while, he'd probably be monitoring my height, weight, and blood pressure. I'd have to wait until everyone was asleep to pack up some food.

"Hi, Mom! Hi, guys!" I hollered as I walked in.

"Jody!" my brothers shouted in unison. I set down my violin and braced myself for impact as Tyler and Kyle thundered down the front hall in their mismatched socks and threw little-brother hugs at me. This was a lot more fun back when they weighed twenty pounds apiece, but I kissed their grimy little heads anyway, thankful that they were ignoring the smell of river water coming from the wet jeans in my bag.

"Hey, Kyle, how was kindergarten? Let's see that loose tooth, Tyler." They ignored me in favor of measuring themselves on tiptoe against my arm, in case they'd grown since breakfast.

"How was music?" Mom called from the kitchen.

"Mmmm," I said, which wasn't lying. I swung my backpack off my shoulder and held it in front of my gym shorts just in time.

Mom stuck her head out of the kitchen door and looked me up and down. "You're a little late."

"Sorry, Mom, we stopped for gelato, and then we, umm, walked down by the river."

"Oh, that's nice, such a pretty day. Did you bring enough money?"

"Yeah, I had some from when I babysat the Smith kids last weekend, remember?" Mom would make such a big deal if she knew Giselle treated. She doesn't believe in that sort of thing at all.

"You're remembering to put half your babysitting money in the bank, right?"

"I know. College." I lifted up Tyler's chin and gave his remaining front tooth a wiggle. "You better get busy on this–college is expensive."

"If I wiggle my toes and they come off, can I get money for 'em?" Kyle asked. He sat down in the hall, yanked off his socks, and got to work on the largest of his toes.

"Don't be gross, Kyle."

"What's college?" Tyler demanded. "Is there bowling?"

"Yes, there's bowling. College is just like an army base but everyone is your same age."

"Whoa!" Tyler was so amazed, he held his body still for an entire ten seconds. "That would be awesome!" Then he got that worried little eyebrow wrinkle that made him look like a tiny old man. He was the most serious seven-year-old I knew. "How many teeth does it take to get in?"

"I'm pretty sure you have just enough," I said, rubbing him on the head. "But you better read a lot of books–tricky ones. Now, who is a big-enough boy to carry my enormous backpack and my violin case full of gold bars?"

"Me! I can! Yes, ma'am!" Kyle and Tyler shouted, snapping off eight or ten salutes each.

"Be careful with them. They weigh five hundred pounds each!"

Kyle grabbed my violin case and was panting and groaning with fake effort before he'd gone three steps.

"Race you!" Tyler said. "Ready, set . . ."

"Don't mess with my stuff!" I hollered after them as they

ricocheted down the hall to my bedroom. "Hey, Mom, mind if I grab a shower before dinner? It was all hot and sweaty on the train." I headed down the hall, hoping she'd stay in the kitchen and not notice that I smelled like sewage.

"Whatever," Mom said. "No rush."

Dad must be working late again. I hustled down to the bathroom before she could see I was wearing my PE shorts. My skin was itchy with tiny red dots where I had been in the river. Looking out the bathroom window, I could see a smudge of pink in the sky to the west. I thought of the soldier watching the same sky from under his bridge, with no way to clean up and no one to make him a warm dinner. Even though it wasn't a cold night, I shivered. A few minutes of hot water and the girl soap Mom kept for just her and me worked wonders. The red spots went away completely, and the lavender smell covered up the river-water stench.

I slipped into my room for pajama pants, socks, and an old army T-shirt of my dad's. I dug my wet jeans and shirt out of my backpack, tossed them into the hamper, and dragged it to the laundry room. Then I put my stinky clothes in the wash with a load of my brothers' jeans and joined Mom in the kitchen.

"Hey, Jody," Mom said. "What do you want with burgers?" Mom was standing with her back to me working a pound of ground beef into patties.

"I don't care. Salad? Peas and carrots? How was your day?"

"Surprisingly quiet," Mom said. She slid the skillet onto

the stove and turned on the heat. "They must have been expecting something that didn't happen. They staffed up the emergency room today and even had the Life Flight helicopter ready to go."

"I wonder what's up," I said. When the base went on alert, Dad always worked a ton of overtime like he'd done last night, but they didn't always put people on extra shifts at the hospital. I opened the fridge and set a head of lettuce and a cucumber on the counter.

"Where's the colander?" I said after I'd checked in all the usual places.

"Sorry, honey. I packed it already."

Mom was an early packer. We weren't moving for two and a half weeks, but she already had a stack of sealed and labeled boxes in the dining room. I could always tell when Dad got PCS orders, because the house smelled like moving boxes. I hated that smell.

"Hey, Mom, some of these oranges are rotten. Do you want me to run them out to the garbage before the boys get into them?"

"Thanks, honey."

I bagged up four perfectly good oranges and took them outside. I set them in a corner of the boot box Mom always kept on the right side of our front door so Dad wouldn't track his muddy boots into the house. I thought about my soldier sitting alone in the dark eating our chocolate bars for dinner. I wondered what the officers who'd tried to kill him were doing. Did they feel guilty? Were they afraid of being caught? They hadn't even posted a lookout or acted very sneaky on the bridge. What made a person so hard-hearted that they just threw a human being away like he was garbage? I hugged my arms across my chest and headed back inside, making a mental list of the things my soldier would need.

"So is it the usual no-Dad routine tonight?" I said when I got back to the kitchen.

"You don't mind, do you?" Mom turned away from the skillet to pop hamburger buns into the toaster.

"Well, what kind of cake did you get?"

"They were all out of chocolate Sachertortes and the kind with cherries, so I got the Mozartkuchen instead."

"With the hazelnuts?"

"And whipped cream." Mom smiled.

She ate sweets when Dad was gone. It was her thing, sweets and reading grocery-store novels in bed. The boys got a story from me instead of Dad, and they got to fall asleep on the sofa. I got to stay up late and listen to any radio station I liked.

Here's the secret I never told anyone: I liked it better when Dad was gone.

After supper, Mom ran a tub and tortured the boys with hot water and soap. I didn't know exactly what went on in there, but it involved four towels, a bucket of toy whales, and a lot of yelling. But at least when I got them on the sofa, they smelled like toothpaste, and they were wearing clean pajamas.

Kyle was first out of the bath, and he always picked *Green Eggs and Ham*. I hated Dr. Seuss! Would it kill the man to use a two-syllable word? But Kyle was the snuggler in the family, and I could put up with the doctor for ten minutes of baby-brother snuggles. Kyle dragged along his old blanky from back when he loved bears more than anything. He was too big for a blanky now, but last Thanksgiving, Dad was in the field and Kyle was missing him really bad. So I sewed an extra set of Dad's name and rank patches to the corner of his blanket. Whenever Dad worked past his bedtime, Kyle got out the blanket, tucked it tight around his body, and carefully traced our name and the three stripes up and three stripes down with a star in the middle for Dad's rank.

I opened up Dr. Seuss, and Kyle wiggled his bony shoulders under my arm and rested his head under my chin. I read and pointed to the words and made him say the last word in each line. I stopped the story to yawn a couple of times toward the end, because it made him sleepy, and then after the story, we prayed. But I secretly changed the words, because what idiot put in the part about dying? Somebody who hates kids, I bet. So we ended the prayer, "If I should sneeze before I wake, oh, what a goopy mess I'd make." Much better. Kyle settled deeper into my lap and twirled his fingers in the ends of my hair. A minute or two later he was making little-boy snores.

Meanwhile, Tyler was at the bookshelf worrying over which of his five hundred volumes of Encyclopedia Brown we should read tonight. Tyler was not a snuggler. When Dad was gone, he slept with Dad's compass hung around his neck on a green bootlace. Tyler handed me *Encyclopedia Brown Gets His Man* and sat at the far end of the sofa. He flipped open the compass and lined it up with true north. He stretched his legs out straight and pressed the bottoms of his bare feet up against mine, because we were secretly sole mates. I would totally not do this, but it was kind of sweet, and he had just had a bath. I read him a mystery, and he told me the solution and every fact in the story that had a clue in it.

When the story was done, Tyler tucked himself in with one of those green army blankets that everyone has a hundred of. He cradled the compass in his hands and took bearings on the TV, the dinner table, the desk, the stack of clean laundry in the corner, and the painting Dad got for Mom in Venice. Sometimes Tyler took forever to fall asleep. Tonight I had to get him out of the way before Dad got home, or I'd never get anything packed. I picked up my science book and read out loud in my sleepiest voice about igneous and metamorphic and sedimentary rocks. In just over ten minutes the magic of science had done its work.

"Did we win?" Mom walked into the living room with another basket of laundry to fold.

I smiled and slid Kyle off my lap. "Victory is ours."

Mom had let her hair down and was wearing her favorite sweats and fluffy socks. "Tea and cake?"

She was in a mood to chat; I could tell.

"Gee, Mom, I'm sorry, but I've got stuff to do for science, and I need to practice tonight, too. Can you just wrap up my half? I'll have it at lunch tomorrow."

"Sure, sweetie." Mom went over to the bookshelf and ran a finger along the row of romance novels. She pulled a paperback from the shelf and set it on the coffee table. She scooped Kyle up off the couch and carried him into the boys' room.

I opened the door to my room, tossed my science book on my desk, and unlatched my violin case. I plucked each of the strings. Figures, Kyle knocked my E string out of tune. I spun the fine tuner to the right, plucking until I heard it hit the right pitch. I tucked the violin under my chin and started in on Pachelbel's Canon. I loved the sound of the piece. In my mind's ear I could hear all three of us playing, Vivian four measures ahead and Giselle an octave lower and four measures behind. I stopped before my favorite part with all the runs of sixteenth notes, because I didn't want to think about never playing that piece together again.

I switched over to the canon I had composed for Giselle and Vivian. I ran through the first violin part thinking of the soldier and why his officers would try to kill him. Dad's known a few mean officers, and one or two lieutenants who weren't very smart, but murder? There had to be something behind it.

I played my canon again a little bit faster. Maybe he'd done something wrong or committed a crime? Or maybe he'd witnessed a crime, and they were covering it up. That's how it would go if this were a movie. I glanced up at my notebook on the music stand. The trickiest part of the composition was coming up. When it was done, I rosined my bow again and flipped pages to the second violin part. Was it against the law for an American to help a Soviet soldier? Could it be like treason or aiding and comforting an enemy? Or maybe it was a crime not to help. Germans had a Good Samaritan law that said you had to stop and give aid if you saw an accident on the road. I couldn't just let him drown, but now what?

When I came to the slow part of my piece, I worked on my vibrato. Maybe tomorrow we could get his side of the story–if he made it through the night. I had to find a few minutes at least to get together some food, but what if Mom decided to stay up for Dad? Then they'd get to talking about whatever was on her mind. They might stay up late and watch the news and the Johnny Carson show. I'd never get anything done.

I switched back to the opening of Pachelbel's Canon and practiced it even slower than the music called for. I projected my sleepiest thoughts into the living room. It worked. After ten minutes, Mom tapped on my door and said, "I'm going to turn in now, Jody. Your cake is in the fridge. Don't stay up too late, sweetie."

"Okay, Mom, good night."

Mission accomplished! I wrapped my violin and bow in a spare pillowcase and slid them under my bed. I tiptoed down the hall and got the box of MREs that we kept in the bottom cupboard for emergencies. There was room for maybe six ready-to-eat meals plus the oranges in my violin case.

What else would he need? I went into the bathroom and rolled up half a roll of toilet paper as small as possible. There was a spare toothbrush in the back of the drawer, and Mom bought Band-Aids in bulk for my brothers, so I snagged a handful plus the sliver of soap that was in the soap dish. I set out a fresh bar so no one would miss it.

What else would a guy with a broken leg want? Duh, something for pain. I got out the bottle of Tylenol, but what he really needed was the Tylenol with codeine that Mom kept locked up. I got the key out of the hiding place in the kitchen and unlocked her rolltop desk. The pain medicine was in the drawer on the right, but my hand froze over a stack of house ads.

Mom must have picked them up from the base housing office. I turned on the desk lamp. Houses, *real* houses, with yards. I flipped through pages and pages of ads. They were all colors, three bedrooms mostly, with garages and gardens. One of them had four bedrooms, and toward the end of the stack there was one with a tree house in the backyard. I would have committed murder to have a tree house of my own when I was seven. That one was in Killeen, Texas. It sounded familiar; there must be an army base nearby.

I took the ad with the tree house over to the bookshelf and got out our American road atlas. I had just found the Texas page when I heard Dad's boots in the stairwell outside. Rats! I dropped the atlas, yanked open the drawer, and grabbed the prescription bottle with the painkillers. I twisted off the cap and dumped the pills into my hand. There were more than a dozen left. I'd better only take seven.

Dad put his key in the lock. I dropped the pills into the top of my left sock, put the rest back into the bottle, and slid the drawer shut just as Dad came in. Shoot, he'd hear me close the rolltop desk. I grabbed a handful of the house pages and ran to sit on the sofa.

"Hey, Jo, thanks for waiting up for me." Dad set his brief-case on the coffee table and collapsed onto the other end of the sofa. He looked terrible. He groaned as he bent over to unlace his boots. "What a long day. Is your mom asleep?"

I nodded. Dad tugged off his polished black boots and pushed them under the coffee table instead of taking them back outside to the boot box. He took his glasses off and rubbed his eyes. His hands were three-pots-of-coffee jumpy.

"Hungry?"

Dad shook his head. He never ate when he was worried. "How was your day?"

I could have told him about the wounded soldier then. I should have. Dad would have fixed everything. He'd saved lives before, twice in Vietnam and once in a training accident last year. It could have all been different. Later, in a room full of very unhappy grown-ups, I said I didn't tell him about the body in the river because he was tired and distracted. That was a lie. I didn't want Dad to fix this for me. I wanted to save that soldier all by myself. I wanted to matter.

"Busy day," I said, which was not technically a lie.

"What have you got there, homework?"

"Um, no, it's houses."

"Hey," Dad said, looking from me to Mom's desk and back. "It was supposed to be a surprise."

"Gee, Dad, I was totally thinking we were going to move into an igloo when you retire. I'm so disappointed now."

I got the look from Dad. Sass was not on the list of things I was allowed to do at home. But actually, so long as I wasn't setting a bad example for the boys or hurting Mom's feelings, Dad kind of liked a snappy answer.

"I never promised no igloos," he said, putting his feet up on the coffee table and closing his eyes.

"Come on, Dad, where is your sense of adventure? None of us has had frostbite yet. You never know, it might be fun."

This was what Dad always said right before all our family catastrophes. He said it before our trip to Seoul, the vomiting capital of South Korea. He said it before we moved to Georgia, the cockroach state. He said it when we moved to Fort Drum and all my clothes and all of my brothers' LEGOs got shipped to Fort Huachuca more than two thousand miles away.

"It is going to be fun," Dad said. "Our own house; we can paint the walls whatever color we want, and Mom can have her garden, and I can have a real workshop in the garage, and the boys can have a dog and a tree house, and..." Dad stopped like he was frozen.

He didn't know what I wanted in my life.

I looked at the real estate ad for the tree-house house in Killeen. Halfway down the page it said Bluebonnet Elementary, Meadowlark Middle School, and South Killeen High School. "I want an orchestra," I blurted out. "Is there an orchestra at the high school?"

"I don't know, Jody, probably. Don't most civilian schools have one?"

"I want to be sure before we pick a house that there's an orchestra."

"I'm sure there will be, and if there isn't, we can find you another music teacher like Herr Müller. That I can promise. You've been happy with him."

"No, I've been happy with my trio. I don't want private lessons anymore, Dad. I want to belong to a real orchestra."

Gee whiz, what got into me? You save one little life and you think you deserve to ask for anything you want.

"Okay, Jody, we'll put orchestra on the list, but you know Tyler wants to move somewhere with dinosaurs, so you've got competition."

"Great." Second fiddle again.

"We have to find a place where I can get a job, Jody. Everything else comes second."

I got up from the sofa. On the way back to my room, I stopped at the bookcase and ran my finger across the green-camouflage volumes of Dad's army manuals.

"Can I take this one to school?" I asked, pulling out the *Army Field Guide to First Aid.*

"Are you planning on injuring someone?"

"Dad!"

"Is something going on?"

"Like what?" I said, praying Dad wasn't a mind reader.

"Like somebody bullying you. Jo, self-defense is your right. If one of those boys at school gives you trouble, you can use those judo moves I showed you."

"Nobody's bothering me, Dad." None of the boys even looked at me at school.

"Well, you should be prepared."

"Can I practice on Ty and Kyle?"

"Those boys are going to be bigger than you someday."

"Not if we stop feeding them now."

Dad laughed, and I took the book back to my room and added it to my already full backpack. I fished my orange Tic Tacs out of the side pocket and dropped the pain pills inside. Then I turned on the Brandenburg Concertos for falling asleep. Now that was music: fifty strings, and wood-winds, too.

Usually I fell asleep trying to sort out the different violin parts. But I kept flashing back to the way my soldier was freezing cold and looked like a wax dummy when I first took him out of the river. I could still smell the sharp tang of sweat and oil on his skin and the bitter taste of river water on his face. When he could finally breathe all on his own, I remembered watching his chest go up and down like he hadn't been almost dead just a few minutes before. I was exhausted, but I kept replaying the moment when I first saw his face. But the more often I remembered it, the less he looked like a grown man with a face full of bruises, and the more he looked like a boy my own age.

When I finally fell asleep, I had the same bad dream I'd been having since I was six. I was walking home from school and every house was exactly the same. The block was endless. I ran faster and faster, but I knew I'd never find my home. Only this time I heard a train and walked down to a river. There was a body in the water, and when I pulled the body out, it was nothing but a skull and bones in an army uniform. I woke up gasping for breath, and the sour smell of the river was in my sweat.

5

Wednesday, May 23, 1990
East Berlin

ALL through the school day on Wednesday, I was hiding smiles, because there is something about having a secret with your friends that livens up even the dullest algebra class. We snuck our homework out of our backpacks so that no one could see they were full of men's clothes and MREs and canteens of water. We shared two lunches among the three of us so that there would be an extra one for our soldier.

After school, Giselle and Vivian and I took the S-Bahn downtown. It was hot and crowded on the train. I thought it would be fun to have an adventure with Vivian and Giselle. We never got together except for music, and they knew lots more kids from the in-crowd than me, so I imagined they were out every weekend at the movies or going shopping or maybe going out for burgers with the basketball boys. But Vivian dove right into her geometry homework as soon as the train got going. Giselle made circle-and-stab moves with her hand against the seat in front of her, like she was fencing a tiny invisible partner. So much for feeling part of the in-crowd.

"Hey, what's the matter?" I said, because miniature fencing was what Giselle did when she was stuck on a test.

"They decided to leave a month early." Giselle stabbed the seat back so hard, the man sitting there turned around and gave her a look. "We were going to spend all of July in Italy and Greece, but they bought a house and now they're in a big hurry to move into it and spend the summer in boring Palo Alto."

"But there are beaches there, right?"

Giselle stabbed at the seat in front of her again. "They have beaches in Italy and Greece. And ruins and sailing and the training camps for the Olympic fencing team."

"Okay."

"Don't you get it, Jody? There's going to be thousands of kids at my new high school. All those other girls will have their California clothes and California boyfriends. But I could have been the girl who spent her summer on the Italian Riviera. At least I'd get some respect for that."

She stabbed the seat in front of her, and when the German turned around again, she gave him the look straight back. Actually, Giselle was pretty much gigantic enough for automatic respect. I'd tell her, but I respected her too much.

Who knew popular girls worried about being popular? I was pretty sure that wherever I got sent for high school, it would be the kind of place where I would get beat up if I mentioned a summer on the Italian Riviera.

"You're going to fit in just fine. You're athletic and you have nice clothes and good jewelry, and your makeup looks perfect every single day. I don't know how you do it. I don't get makeup at all."

"You don't even need makeup," Giselle said. "Look at you. Perfect skin. Not a zit in sight. How do you manage that, huh?"

"Umm ... the zits take one look at all these freckles and figure they can't compete?" I smiled and gave her a little nudge on the shoulder, because honestly, it's the nicest thing anyone has ever said about my looks. Ever.

"You should try it sometime. A little peachy lipstick and something dramatic around your eyes, you could be a movie star. Don't you think, Vivi?"

Vivian set her pencil down and looked at me over the tops of her glasses. "I can't stand the competition already."

"Not much danger of that," I said. "Mom would give me the five-hour feminism lecture if I went out of the house in makeup. I'm not allowed until next year and then only on special occasions."

"Image is power, honey. That's what my mom taught me," Giselle said.

"Potsdamer Platz," Vivian called, and we all grabbed our stuff and piled off the train. It was just as warm outside, but at least there was a breeze.

We retraced our steps to the river. I started looking for our soldier as soon as we could see the bridge ahead, but he wasn't where we'd left him yesterday. What if those officers had come back and killed him again? What if they'd killed him and left the body?

But he was there. He had pulled branches around him and was lying completely still, with the green army towels covering him up. If I hadn't known where to look, he would have been invisible. He watched us as we walked up.

"Have returned," he said. His voice was low and groaning. He rolled to his side to face us. Except for not being dead, he looked worse than yesterday. His black eyes were puffier. There was a purple bloom of bruises around his ribs peeking out from below Giselle's PE shirt. His broken foot was back pointing in the right direction, but there was a bulge over the top of his boot that was almost twice the size of his other leg.

"Hey there," Giselle said.

I could see she was going to say something else, but it just occurred to me that we didn't even know his name. He could be anybody. The soldier pushed himself up on one elbow. He opened his mouth to say something, but then his face turned gray. He broke out into a sweat.

"He's going to faint," I said. "Look at him. It's probably the pain." I walked a little closer. He had spread his uniform pants and shirt on the ground to dry, and he had taken a branch and made a splint of it. He'd tied it over his boot using the bootlace from his other foot. Thank God! I'd read up on broken legs in Dad's FM 5-22 during math. The section about how to set broken bones had made my stomach go wobbly just looking at the pictures.

"How is it?" I pointed to his splinted leg.

"Is only pain. I breathe in. I breathe out." He looked at me and then Vivian and Giselle and then he looked back at me again. "You are same angel from yesterday?"

"Communists don't believe in angels." I reached into my pocket for the Tic Tac box I'd used to hide the codeine. I emptied the whole thing into my palm and sorted out the bright orange candies from the dull orange pills. "I brought something for the pain, but you have to eat it with food, or it will hurt your stomach."

He looked at me like I was the Second Coming of Jesus. Like my brothers looked at Dad when he said we could get a puppy when he retired. "You are angel of life," he said to me solemnly.

"One," I said in a serious voice. "You can only take one of these. It's very strong. It's four-thirty now, so you can have another when the sun comes up, and the last one when the sun goes down tomorrow. That will be about twelve hours apart."

He reached out and took three pills from my hand like they were sacred things and swallowed one down dry. I un-latched my violin case and took out the canteen and the brown-foil-wrapped field MREs. The soldier reached for the water and drained half the canteen in one long swallow. "There's a whole meal in each one of these packages," I said. "You don't have to heat it up or anything. They don't look nice but they taste okay, and they keep without a fridge." I handed him a slightly squashed peanut butter and jelly sandwich. "But eat this now. It's my lunch, and it will be gross if you don't."

He turned the package over three times and then handed it back to me. "Is opened?"

"Like this." I showed him how to pull apart the Ziploc.

"Un. Believable!" Giselle whispered to Vivian. "They can build a nuclear missile system, but they can't open a sandwich."

The soldier took a deep smell of peanut butter plus strawberry jam. He ate my sandwich in two bites.

"Ugh! Chew with your mouth closed," Vivian said.

The soldier went right on gulping down his food and sucking the last bits of Wonder Bread off his teeth. Vivian shuddered and said, "Were you cold last night?" She opened her violin case and took out a pair of jeans, a T-shirt, and a button-front shirt.

"For me?"

"For you."

"Why so kind to a stranger?"

"Because it's the right thing to do," Giselle said firmly. "Because we are all Americans here. This is what we do—we help people."

The soldier looked from the stack of clothes in Vivian's hand to the pile of MREs on the ground.

"Go on," Vivian said. "Get dressed." She turned and walked down to the bank of the river, and Giselle followed her.

I was about to follow them, but then I turned back. "What's your name?" I asked.

"I am called Arvo Kross."

"Arvo? That doesn't sound Russian."

"Is Estonian name."

"Estonia? Never heard of it. Is that a country, or is it a tribe of people, like Zulu or something?"

"It is my home and maybe soon it will be my country."

"Isn't the Soviet Union your country?" I pointed at his uniform still lying on the ground.

"Never!" He kicked dirt over his uniform jacket with his good leg like he was spitting on the flag. "They claim me, but I will never claim them."

I couldn't even imagine one of Dad's soldiers talking like that, not even the ones who don't like the army. "Okay, Arvo, from . . ."

"Estonia."

"Right. I'll just let you get dressed." I went to sit with the girls. Giselle was throwing rocks into the water.

"His name is Arvo," I said.

"Arvo, hmm," Vivian said.

"Yeah, Arvo Kross from someplace called Estonia. Have you heard of it?"

"Yeah," Vivi said. She drew a map in the air with her finger. "It's in the top corner of Europe, next to Russia and under Finland." Vivian had won the geography bee three years running and also the spelling bee. If there was an algebra bee, she'd be the international champ. The boys in our class called her Queen Bee except when Giselle was standing right there.

"Thank goodness he speaks English," Giselle said. "Maybe he can explain why his officers are trying to kill him. I couldn't sleep last night thinking about it. Officers just aren't like that."

Says the daughter of a general, I thought. Giselle looked at my look and added, "Because they need to have the trust of their enlisted men or they'd never follow orders. It's stupid to abuse a soldier. Officers are always outnumbered."

She did have a point. "I wonder if he'll even tell us the truth," I said. "Soviets aren't exactly known for being straight up with each other, let alone us evil Westerners."

"I've heard some pretty crazy rumors at the consulate about how things are in the Soviet Union these days," Vivian said. "The *Morgenpost* says there won't be enough apartments or even barracks for the soldiers to live in once they get home."

I picked up a stone and skipped it three hops across the

slow-moving surface of the Spree. We were quiet for a few minutes, and I could hear Arvo struggling with the clothes. "Thank you," Arvo called when he was done changing. We climbed back up the riverbank to where he was sitting. He looked much less pathetic in men's clothes.

Giselle's PE clothes were folded in a tidy pile. He was turning over his uniform and smoothing it out so the other side would dry. "You have a name?" he said to me.

"Yes–" Vivian barged in. She introduced herself and Giselle and then me.

"Thank you," Arvo said, looking at each of us in turn. "Thank you for food and clothing and very much thank you for medicine. I am much better now."

He did look a lot better. He wasn't so pale, and he didn't guard his body stiffly like people do when they are in pain. Codeine must be pretty amazing stuff. No wonder Mom kept it locked up.

"What happened to you?" I said. "Why were those men trying to kill you? We saw the whole thing; they were officers."

"You are needing whole story. Please sit down."

Giselle picked up her PE clothes and made a cushion of them to sit on a boulder, and Vivian and I sat side by side on an old railroad tie. Arvo folded the army towels and put them under his foot to elevate it.

"First thing you girls learn in school about the Soviet Union is that we are your enemy. It is not true. We are our

66

own enemy. I am no Russian. Estonia is my home. I am alone in the Soviet Army. I am the only one from Estonia in Berlin, and they hate me for it. They spit in my food. They steal my letters to my family and the money I send to them. They never speak to me but to curse. For years I took this as a blind man takes the dark. It has always been so for Soviet soldiers who are not Russian. But I can see now. With the glasnost there is truth about our history in our own newspapers. We didn't ask the Russians to come; they conquered us."

"Everyone knows that!" Vivian said.

"Really? Everyone?" I said. Vivi had a talent for making me feel like a second grader.

"Yeah, well, everyone who's read ahead in the high school western civ book."

"It's the whole reason we're here in Germany," Giselle added. "To keep you Soviets from gobbling up Germany and Denmark and all the rest of these little countries."

"This is all news in Estonia, in the whole Soviet Union," Arvo said. "Our history books said the whole world was longing to be Communist. There would only be peace and freedom when the whole world was Communist."

"Seriously?" I said. "Because even I know that's a lie."

"Now we all know. Last summer we made the Baltic Way, a chain of two million people who held hands from my city, Tallinn, to Riga to Vilnius—six hundred kilometers. We stood together in a line to ask for independence. We are almost free, and I want to be home in my own country when we are finally free. Home..."

And then he stopped, because he was almost going to cry. And I thought, I love my country the same as anyone, but there isn't any place in America that's home to me. And then I thought, Never mind that he was almost murdered yesterday; Arvo's a lucky man.

He turned to Giselle and said, "It is because of your Martin Luther King and Gandhi, too. We read about them, and we try not to seek revenge on our Russian neighbors who stole our houses and jobs and cars. We try to stand up for justice with no violence. I want to be there. I want to be with my family making my country free."

"Can't you get a transfer?" Giselle said. "You're just a translator. They could get someone else to do your work."

"Is not so easy," Arvo said. "I asked the only officer who was ever kind to me, but he said no. Then the lieutenants you saw on the bridge punished me for asking to go home." He pushed up his shirtsleeve. There were clusters of round pink scars up and down his arm that were still puffy and new. "Cigarettes," Arvo said.

I wrapped my arms around my knees and hugged them to my chest, but I couldn't look away. "They tortured you?" I said. "Why? My dad would go to jail if he did this to a soldier of his. He'd go to jail even if he did this to an enemy soldier."

"Three days ago they changed their minds. They said I could go and serve my last years of duty in Estonia."

"But there was a catch," Vivian said.

"A catch?"

"You had to do something for them, something bad," Vivi said.

"Yes, I must carry a package on a train to Istanbul and then to Baghdad, a dangerous package, too dangerous for their own Russians to carry."

"Like a bomb?" I said.

"A poison. A gas. If it broke open, it would kill everyone for kilometers in every direction."

"Oh my gosh," I said. "We have to tell my dad."

"We have to tell *my* dad," Giselle said. "Poison gas—on the train—that's crazy!"

"No!" Arvo shouted. "Please! No." He quieted his voice and looked up at the bridge and then back at the road. "I tried. I told them two days ago."

"How? Who did you tell?" Giselle barged in.

"I am translator. I have radio. I contacted the American army. They promised to help. I traded my freedom for their poison gas. But I was betrayed. My officers found out, and they beat me. If not for you angels, I would be a dead man."

"The HAZMAT trucks at the motor pool last night and the overtime at the hospital—that was all for you," I said. "Arvo, you have to come back to Zehlendorf with us. They're looking for you! They'll be so glad we found you!"

"No, listen to me! They betrayed me. You angels, what do you know of the world? There is a spy, a Soviet spy. Bring me to the Americans, and he will know!"

"So?" Giselle said. "We aren't going to give you to him. You'll be fine. We'll keep you safe."

"I am nothing. If I go with you, they will know. They will find my mother and sister. They will make them suffer."

"What?" Vivi said.

"In the Soviet Union people disappear. A car comes in the night, and people are gone forever."

"Like to Siberia? Like in the movies?"

"Yes, just like that. Please, my sister is a schoolgirl like you. How could I let something–anything–happen to her?"

Arvo looked at me, and he had that worried wrinkle in his forehead just like Tyler gets. I spent about two seconds imagining my brothers in Siberia.

"I won't tell," I said. "I promise."

I looked at Vivian, and she slowly nodded her head, but Giselle was still thinking.

"Look, I know Communism is bad, but how can you be this bad to your own people? It doesn't make sense," she said.

"Communism written down in books seems very sensible," Arvo said. "Everyone gives what they are able to give. Everyone gets what they need. No one is rich, but no one is poor. It seems like a good idea. But it doesn't work! There is corruption from the smallest town to the largest city. A few men in power live like kings and the rest of us are the paupers of the world." He looked from Giselle to me to Vivian. "How can I make you understand? America is a charmed country. You have laws *and* policemen who obey the laws. You have grocery stores *and* food in them all the time. You can read whatever book or newspaper you choose." He paused and looked at the ground. "You can say the truth and not be afraid. Do you know the price of that?"

"They would actually put your family in jail if we brought you to the American army base?" Giselle said.

"I could name one hundred people from the neighborhood where I grew up. Gone. Not to jail–to hard labor, to the mines."

The mines. I shuddered. The mines were the reason Dad left West Virginia and joined the army. They were the reason I don't have a grandpa. "Giselle–please!" I said.

She searched Arvo's face, and I couldn't guess what she was thinking. Between the split and swollen lip and the two black eyes, he was not the most reliable-looking person. But then Giselle looked at me.

"I promise," she said, and I hugged her.

Arvo breathed in deeply and put his hand over his heart. "Thank you. Thank you. I will hide. I will hide like the Forest Brothers from the old days."

"Forest Brothers? What are you talking about?" Vivi said.

"The Forest Brothers are the Estonian Robin Hood.

They hid in the woods, and they fought for our freedom. My foot will get better, and I will find a path to get home even if I have to walk the whole way."

"How?" Giselle said. "You don't have money; you don't have a passport, a map, a clue. You've got nothing."

Arvo sat up a little straighter even though I could tell it hurt him to do it. He looked Giselle in the eye in a way people don't when she's sounding bossy and said, "I have myself. That is not nothing."

Something about the way he said that simple thing tugged at me.

"You've got us," I said. "We'll help."

The Tiergarten, West Berlin

We walked back toward the Brandenburg Gate. My violin case felt odd with no weight in it, and we were unusually quiet. The golden afternoon light on the buildings along Unter den Linden made them seem a little less grimy than yesterday. You could see from the fancy brickwork that it had once been the upscale part of town. That made it even more depressing to see all the empty storefronts and shabby upstairs apartments. It was the middle of rush hour, and the thought of spending almost an hour crammed into a commuter train with a bunch of crabby people in suits wasn't very appealing.

"Let's walk through the Tiergarten and catch the S-Bahn home on the far side," I said.

Vivi nodded, and Giselle led the way under the Brandenburg Gate, across the traffic-packed Ebertstrasse, and into the long shady blocks of the park. We walked through the south side of the Tiergarten, past the playground and the goldfish pond. We could still hear the rush-hour traffic, but there was shade and grass and, best of all, no one to over-hear us.

"What are we going to do about Arvo?" Vivian said quietly. "Do you think he'll be okay on his own?"

"We have to help him," I said. I swung my empty back-pack off my shoulder and took out the box of Tic Tacs. "It doesn't matter if his broken foot gets better–without money and a passport, he's stuck." I handed the candy to Vivi. She waved it away, but Giselle took some.

"I don't know," Giselle said, popping the Tic Tacs into her mouth. "He said he'd be fine. What if that story he told us isn't true? What if he's a criminal or something? And what if it's against the law for us to help him? My dad would freak if I broke the law."

"I wish there was someplace safe we could take him," Vivian said. "But I think he's right about whoever helps him needing to give him back to the Soviet army. If we don't help him escape secretly, I don't think anyone else will."

I thought about Arvo sitting under that bridge with nothing but the little bit of food and clothes we gave him. My mind jumped to Tyler because Arvo was a lot like him, all serious. What if Tyler was hurt and alone in some other country far from home where no one knew how smart and kind he was or that he was afraid of the dark? I hadn't even thought to bring Arvo a flashlight.

"We can't just leave him there," I said. "Not when he doesn't have anyone else." I paused while a group of moms with strollers passed us on their way to the playground. "Maybe we can't get him all the way to Estonia, but there has to be a way to get him out of East Berlin."

Vivian swerved right, onto a path that led to the busy street with the Siegessäule in the middle and the big golden lady on the top of the pillar. Lots of tourists were out taking pictures, and there were sausage vendors all around. She went to the newspaper stand.

"*Eine Zeitung, bitte,*" she said.

Vivian brought back the *Berliner Morgenpost* and scanned the headlines. "I wonder if anyone has reported about this."

"What?" I said. I glanced over Vivian's shoulder. "No one knows he's there. How could it be in the paper?"

Vivian flipped through the first dozen pages. "Arvo is missing from his unit, right? The Russians who threw him off the bridge think he's dead, but everyone else must think he ran away."

No wonder Vivian got a hundred percent on every quiz at school, because I never would have thought of that.

"Those officers will be waiting for somebody to find the body," Vivian went on. "If it doesn't turn up somewhere along the river, they're going to start searching for it, and I bet they'll begin right from the spot they heaved him into the water."

"Oh my gosh," Giselle said. "We need a plan."

I started walking toward the S-Bahn station on the west end of the park. "So we need to move the body of an almost, but not quite, dead guy. How are we going to do that? Carry him? Toy wagon? Wheelchair?"

The glass dome over the hippo habitat started to show above the trees. I swerved onto a path going south to take us around the zoo. I could smell the sharp, sour fish smell from the penguin exhibit.

"I don't know, Jody," Giselle said. "A moving target is the easiest thing to find. What if we just hid him where he is? He was hard to see today all wrapped up in green and hiding under that bush, and we knew exactly where to look for him."

"Maybe," I said. "They would be looking for a dead body, so probably they'd only look along the bank and not up under the bridge."

"He might be fine for a while under the bridge, but there's no way he's going to get all the way to Estonia with no money and no paperwork," Vivian said.

We walked on a little farther, past the pond with flamingos. Eventually the fishy smells of animal feed were replaced with the smell of fried pork and mustard from the bratwurst cart that always stood by the zoo entrance.

"What we need is an excuse for a grown-up to travel with three kids who are obviously too old to be his kids," Giselle said.

I frowned and kicked at the gravel on the path. "What we need is something like a school field trip."

We came out of the park and headed toward the S-Bahn

station. There was a record store, and we all automatically stopped and looked in the window at a bunch of mannequins with pink and orange Mohawks and black leather jackets. There was an album cover from U2 and one from Madonna and one from the Bangles. The Bangles were my favorite because they were an all-girl band.

An all-girl band. I stood stock-still, hardly daring to taste the idea. I closed my eyes. Could it actually work?

"We need something like our music teacher, Herr Arvo Kross, taking his string trio to the Solo and Ensemble Contest in Paris this Friday."

Vivi and Giselle turned from the window and just looked at me. I got chills.

We headed toward the train and walked the last block very slowly. We didn't say anything so as not to spoil the perfectness of the idea. By the time we came to the station, we were grinning like fools.

"Oh my gosh, could we really make this work?" Vivian almost whispered. "Could we save Arvo *and* still get our trip to Paris?"

I nodded. We turned to Giselle.

"I am not giving up on Paris," she said. "We'll never play together again if we don't go. We worked hard on our piece, and we could win this year, you know we could!"

"We could win," Vivi said. "And we could be in Paris! Just us. No diplomats to meet. No stupid receptions like we have every time I travel with my mom."

Just us and music, I thought. One perfect weekend before I leave Germany forever.

"We can do this," I said. "We have to do this. Arvo needs us. We're the only ones who can save him, right?"

They both agreed.

"Okay, so we just need to . . . ummm . . ."

"Tell a whole bunch of lies?" Vivi said.

"Yeah." I thought about my mom and dad and about how much they trusted me. Setting a good example for my brothers was like a religion with them.

"They'll never know," Vivi said. She steered us to the shady end of the train platform. "They'll think we are at the competition with Herr Müller, and we will be at the competition–just with Arvo. It's almost like we're not lying–right? We go. We play music in the morning. We help Arvo find some other Estonians in Paris in the afternoon, and then we go home on Sunday just like they are expecting. What could possibly go wrong?"

Clearly, we had no idea.

"You know," Giselle said, "I don't think my parents even think about me when I'm not there. They're so busy all the time. As long as I'm with people they know, doing things they approve of, they don't care. I think they're kind of glad I'll be gone over the weekend. Dad never thinks of anything but his command, even when he has a day off, and Mom works full-time plus overtime just with the stuff an officer's wife has to do. They want me to go."

"Mom got me francs from the bank on Monday," I said. "She got me film for my camera. She'd be sad for me if I couldn't go."

"We'll go!" Vivi said. "It's only a little bit of lying."

"It's lying for a good reason." Giselle let her backpack slide off her shoulder and hit the platform with a thump. "Arvo will never make it on his own. Walk to Estonia? Right! He can fly to Estonia from Paris."

"Vivi, you said there were Estonian people in Paris," I said. "Are you sure? Where are they?"

"I don't know exactly," Vivi said. "But Paris is packed with immigrants. I bet we can find someone who knows where people from the Baltics live. Probably those people will give Arvo a place to stay and help him earn enough money to fly home. It won't be fast, but it will be way safer than walking."

"I'll lie to save someone's life," I said.

"It's not like our parents are going to be worried," Giselle said. "All we have to do is get on a train. How hard can that be?"

Thursday, May 24, 1990
Downtown West Berlin

The next day, just Giselle and I went to see Arvo under the bridge. It was Vivian's ballet day and not Giselle's fencing day. I wouldn't have cared if it was my have-tea-with-the-Queen-of-England-day; I was dying to see Arvo again. I'd had the most awful dream of those officers coming back and beating him up all over again and then taking him somewhere where I couldn't find him. I brought fresh water bottles, a little bit of cash, and a flashlight in case he was afraid of the dark. Giselle brought the crutches she'd used last year, a dress shirt that belonged to Vivian's dad, and a belt and a navy blue tie, so he would have something to wear that made him look like a music teacher. We didn't bring our instruments, and we went to the bridge by a different route to not attract attention. I totally felt like a spy.

Arvo loved our idea of going to Paris. And he knew just how to find Estonians there. Apparently they were all Lutherans before Communism made believing in God illegal, so if we could find a Lutheran church in Paris, then we could eventually find escaped Estonians who would help him get home. Arvo explained all this while he practiced with Giselle's crutches. He did okay, even on the slope.

"He looks kind of scruffy," I said to Giselle as we sat under the bridge and watched.

"Scruffy?" Giselle said. "He looks like a cheap drunk with a bad haircut who just shook hands with the wrong end of a bar fight. We have got to do something about that man's face."

Arvo's black eyes had blossomed from reddish blue to greenish yellow, and although both eyes were less puffy, the dark marks were twice as large. He had cleaned the blood away from where his lip was split, but he had three days of very uneven beard growing. It was not a music teacher look.

"Arvo," Giselle said, "we need to go shopping."

He hobbled up on the crutches. "Yes, I am looking . . ." I could see him searching for a nicer word than "revolting."

"You need to look tidy," I said, "like a music teacher. We need a razor and I guess—"

"Deodorant," Giselle barged in.

I was not going to say that out loud. "Umm, would you like a comb?"

Arvo nodded.

"And I hate to say it, but I think you are going to need some makeup."

"Lots of makeup," Giselle said. "Come on, girl, we need to go to the KDW."

I trailed after Giselle up the riverbank. We stopped in the

bushes to make sure the road was empty and then headed toward the Kaufhaus des Westens in the busy shopping part of the Kurfürstendamm.

Shopping with Giselle was a revelation. She walked into the store like she owned it. She never compared prices, and she had an opinion about everything. Leather jackets—hot. Spike heels—not worth the trouble. Levi's with rips and tears already in them—so last year. Blue mascara—please! We filled up a basket with the things Arvo needed to get cleaned up.

"Makeup!" Giselle announced, striding in the direction of the bright lights and mirrors in the cosmetics section of the department store. "I have no idea what you white people use." She breezed past a cluster of German grandmas, oblivious to their disapproving clucks, and took up space at the makeup counter.

"Oh. Umm . . ." I loved Giselle, but sometimes she made me feel like a little kid. "I'm not much of a makeup expert. I really have no idea what we should buy."

"Seriously?"

"None."

"Girl, you have got to stop shopping with your mom."

"Okay." I liked shopping with my mom.

"Promise me you'll shop with your girlfriends when you get to your new school." Giselle sat me down on a tall pink stool at the makeup counter and motioned for one of the ladies in a pink smock to come over and wait on us.

I tried to imagine myself in one of those American malls I'd heard my cousins talk about.

"Your mom wants you to be pretty and she doesn't," Giselle went on. "Moms are like that. It's because they all just turned forty."

"Guten Tag. Kann ich euch helfen?" the makeup lady said.

"Jody needs a new look," Giselle said.

"Yes, I see." The makeup lady switched to English like flipping radio stations. It would take me forever to get that good at German. She had perfect hair and perfect makeup. Even in her dorky pink smock, I could imagine her modeling for a magazine. I tucked my grubby tennis shoes underneath the stool and felt even more like a second grader. "Some pink for the cheeks," the makeup lady said. "And for the eyes–"

"She needs foundation," Giselle said firmly. "The really good kind. For when she gets zits."

I could have died right there.

"What a shame! Such lovely skin even with the freckles," the makeup lady said.

I bet she never had a zit in her life.

"Do you suffer in your cycle?"

I was never going to shop for makeup ever again. I closed my eyes and thought about Arvo and all the bruises on his face. "Yes," I said. "I suffer a lot."

She gave me some makeup that felt exactly like the school paste I used in kindergarten and smelled like insect repellent.

I think Giselle felt a little bit sorry for me, because she bought me the brightest red nail polish in the store. On the way back to the bridge, we got a timetable for the train and a tourist map of Berlin to help Arvo find us at the Spandau Bahnhof on Friday.

The next day my classes felt like they were five hundred years long. We spent all day listening to people give their dreams and goals speeches. Yawn. But the whole time I was listening, I was thinking how fun it would be to give a real dreams and goals speech.

"Yes, my goal is to run away to Paris with my two best friends and a complete stranger. We plan to enter a music contest, win it, become world-famous musicians, live our whole lives in fancy hotels all over Europe, and eat gelato every day."

Very tempting, but it would ruin everything, so I gave the speech I had written. "I love music, and I want to be a music teacher when I grow up." Not my dream exactly, more of a plan if nothing better worked out. Aunt Cassandra was a piano teacher. She raised chickens and cousins and lots of vegetables that she put in jars and sent to us for holidays. She lived in a little town where the big event every week was the high school game. To be fair, she seemed perfectly happy, but I didn't want a little life. I just chose music teacher for my speech because it's a goal that makes grown-ups think you are a responsible person.

After school Giselle's and Vivian's folks dropped them

off at my apartment at four o'clock exactly, because when you're an army family, being late is one of the seven deadly sins. They hugged us and took our picture together. Usually I hate having my picture taken, but the only way we were going to get dropped off at the station was if we were running late. Otherwise, Mom would insist on coming in and handing us over to Herr Müller and watching the train leave. Giselle, Vivi, and I agreed the whole trick was going to be getting to the Spandau Bahnhof late, but not so late we missed the train.

"Okay, girls, let's pack up your stuff and get in the van," Mom said as soon as the other parents had gone. It was only ten after four.

"Quick," I whispered to Giselle. "We need to stall for time. Get my brothers wound up!"

Giselle knew just what to do. "Climb aboard, cowboy," she said. She knelt down so that Tyler could climb on her back.

"I'm not a cowboy. I'm a cavalry scout," Tyler insisted as he locked his arms around Giselle's neck and squeezed.

"Okay, soldier, hold on!" Giselle galloped in long-legged strides around the coffee table and down the hall.

"I'm a cowboy! Me!" Kyle shouted, tugging at the leg of my jeans.

"Vivi's a much better pony than me, Kyle." Vivian took the hint and made *clip-clop* sounds with her Keds and shook her silky, straight hair. Kyle climbed up on a chair and petted her mane. She made a horsey sound, scooped Kyle onto her back, and galloped after Giselle.

"Bang! Bang!" Kyle shouted, shooting Tyler with his finger. "Gotcha!"

"No way! Giddyup, Giselle!" Tyler yelled.

Mom watched for a moment as they galloped around the coffee table and back down the hall, and then she said, "You know those boys are going to vomit if you get them all wound up."

Giselle froze and Vivi's mouth dropped right open. The game was over in a nanosecond.

While Mom was distracted, I took her keys off the hook by the front door and hid them under the pile of everybody's shoes on the floor—poor Mom. We all spent the next fifteen minutes being helpful and concerned and looking everywhere for the lost keys, but the whole time I was thinking about Arvo. Was he okay? Did the Russians find him? What if he didn't make it to the station? I kept an eye on the clock, and when it was four-thirty, I kicked the shoes to the side and shouted, "Here they are, Mom! They fell in a shoe."

Mom didn't exactly say a swear—but she was thinking one; I could tell. We were all out the door and in the van in less than a minute, and Mom took off. Kyle bounced around in his car seat and made siren noises. It's what he did to help Mom drive fast. Tyler took out the very tattered and sticky street map of Berlin and started calling out directions to the zoo, which was his favorite place to go. Mom squeezed the steering wheel very tightly and took many calming breaths.

It wasn't fair. She was the kind of mom you could talk to. If I had told her three days ago that Herr Müller had canceled our trip, maybe she would have figured out how to skip her shifts at the hospital and packed up the brothers and taken us to Paris herself. But I didn't want her to come. Next fall I'd have to go to whatever school she and Dad picked, and it was probably going to be one of those monster schools with eight thousand kids. And I'd live in a house they chose, in a town they wanted to live in, and go to the church they thought was best. Dad said that when we moved, I could paint my room any color I wanted except black—like I cared about the color of my room. I wanted to save Arvo from those men who tried to kill him. I wanted him to be free. I wanted to play music with my friends, and I wanted to go to Paris, not for a family vacation but just for me.

Still, I couldn't help feeling sorry for Mom. When we got to the train station, she said, "Better hop out and run for it, girls, I'll never find parking in time."

I gave Mom a kiss, which I usually don't, and said, "Really, Mom, thanks for driving us. Thanks for everything." And I meant it.

Giselle and Vivian had already unloaded the violins and the cello, and they were running past the bright yellow U-Bahn entrance and into the main train station. There was a big old-fashioned clock in the middle of the station where we had agreed to meet, and I scanned the crowds looking for Arvo. All I could see were strangers, and my heart sank. They found him, I thought. Those officers came back and took him away and I'll never see him again. But then a skinny man with crutches and a very short mustache started walking toward us. He was wearing jeans and a gray T-shirt that said ARMY across the front in big black letters. I had to look three times to be sure it was him. The black eye and bruises were completely covered up with makeup; the mustache hid most of the cut on his mouth.

"Hey! You made it!" I said, and I wanted to hug him, but then it seemed like a silly idea, so I didn't.

"Come on, let's get tickets," I said. "We only have a few minutes." We stood in line, and Vivian counted out the marks for our train fare and handed them to Arvo.

"Oh, look! A spy guy!" Giselle said. She pointed to a man in a black turtleneck sweater and hat, and she slugged me on the shoulder.

"Think OPSEC!" I said, and slugged her back.

It was our version of the slug bug game. Whenever we were riding the commuter train to our lesson or walking around Berlin, we'd look for a German who was dressed in a black turtleneck sweater just like the spy on Armed Forces TV. There were army commercials on it all the time, and a bunch of them were designed to warn soldiers and their families not to blab about army stuff in front of civilians and foreigners. In the commercials, the spy was always a foreign-looking guy in a hat and black turtleneck, and the spot always ended with the catchy slogan "Think OPSEC," for Operational Security. The main result of the ads was that none of us would ever dream of wearing a black turtleneck in public.

Arvo was the next in line. I got a nervous wobble in my stomach thinking about what would happen if we got caught. It wasn't like me to be sneaky. I couldn't even remember the last time I'd lied to my mom about anything bigger than who'd eaten the last cookie.

"Drei Jugend und ein Erwachsener Fahrkarte bis Paris, bitte."

We all tried not to look guilty, but the ticket seller handed him three youth tickets and one adult ticket without a single question. It was almost disappointing. We ran up the escalator just as the train pulled into the station. Arvo trailed behind. We caught our breath as a few dozen passengers got off. I glanced back and the spy guy in the black sweater was getting off the escalator. Was he following us? No, I thought, I'm being paranoid. He's a normal German in black clothes. Lots of people wear black.

Vivian took the tickets from Arvo and looked at the car number on them. "This way," she said. "We need the first four cars on this train. The cars in the back are going to Amsterdam and Copenhagen." We ran after her past three more cars to the one with the number that matched our ticket. Arvo lagged behind. His face was gray and he was sweating a lot.

"Giselle, wait!" I called as she disappeared into a train car.

"Come on, hurry!" Vivian said. She sprang into the car

and leaned out the door. I looked back. Arvo had stopped entirely. He stood head down with his arms dangling over his crutches.

"Here, take these," I said to Vivian, handing over my backpack and violin. I hurried back to where he was standing. "Don't stop now, Arvo. You're almost there."

He looked up, but he was too out of breath to speak. I stepped closer and whispered, "Get on that train and you'll be free. Those officers will never find you."

Arvo nodded, still looking down. I tugged at his shirt to get him to stand up straight. I took his crutches and held them in one hand. Then I pulled his arm over my shoulder so we could walk side by side.

"It's only twenty steps." This trick always worked with my brothers. "One, two, three." We started moving forward.

"Chiteeree, pyatt."

"Six, seven, eight."

"Devyet, deysyet."

The train whistle sounded.

"Jody!" Vivian yelled, still leaning out the door.

"Almost there, almost there," I whispered to Arvo. He kept on counting. I could see the spy guy walking toward us quickly, and he wasn't even looking at train car numbers. He was staring at us. We came to the door, and Giselle reached out and tugged Arvo up by the front of his shirt. He gasped in pain. I gave him a shove from behind just as the train made its first lurch forward. Giselle took Arvo and set him up against the wall beside the door. I climbed aboard, and as the doors slid shut, I looked back at the platform. The spy guy was jumping onto the train two cars down from ours.

We were, all four of us, plus our instruments, packed into a space no bigger than my apartment closet. Through the window in front of us I could see rows of second-class seats, and behind us were the bathrooms and the oversize luggage compartment.

"We made it," Giselle said, still holding Arvo by both shoulders because he looked like he was going to faint.

"What happened? Are you okay?" I said.

He was still breathing hard, and sweat ran down his face. "*Da,* walking–okay. Running–not so good for me."

"Right. Well, let's just make a note of that." Vivian turned to me. "No running. Write that down, Jody, and probably no jumping or dancing either. A lot of fun you're going to be, Arvo. I don't think we're ever going to take you on vacation with us again."

Arvo gave her a nervous look, but Giselle let out a laugh so loud, half the passengers in second class turned around to look at us. And then I got an attack of nervous giggles, and Vivian, who is not the giggling type, laughed so hard she had to cross her legs and squeeze her knees together. Five minutes later, we were all three sitting on the floor gasping for breath and still laughing. Arvo was not nearly as pale as before, but he was looking more worried about us by the minute.

"Perhaps we should sit down," he said when there was the tiniest pause.

"Actually, Arvo—we are sitting down," I said, and Giselle let out another huge laugh, and we were off giggling again. Even at the time, I thought, Every time I go on a vacation, this is what I'm going to remember—sitting on the floor with my friends in the doorway of a train laughing myself to tears and giddy with relief and anticipation.

Friday, May 25, 1990
The Night Train to Paris

We laughed clear out of the station, and then I remembered the man in the black turtleneck.

"Hey, guys," I said. "Do you remember the spy guy from the station? Do you think he could be following us? He was looking at us, and he got onto the train at the very last minute."

"Huh," Giselle said, looking up. "Arvo, is someone going to come looking for you when they discover you are missing from your unit? In America it's the MPs who hunt down missing soldiers. Do you think the Soviet MPs are looking for you?"

"I don't think the spy guy's an MP," I said. "Military police always work in pairs, and he was alone, plus no uniform."

"I was followed," Arvo said. "I left the bridge last night in the dark. I crossed under the Brandenburg Gate and hid in the park. This morning I went to the S-Bahn. A man there followed me, so I went to a store instead. In the bathroom, I shaved and used the makeup. I bought a cap. I went back to the S-Bahn, but the man was still there looking at people getting on board."

"Someone followed you? Oh my gosh, Arvo, who would follow you?" Vivian said.

"KGB."

"What? No way! In Germany?" I said.

"Wait, how could you tell the guy was Russian?" Vivian said. "He could be anyone, right?"

"He had poor shoes," Arvo said.

"Poor shoes? You have got to be kidding!" Giselle looked up at him from the floor where we were still sitting.

"No, it's true," Vivian said. "Russians have clunky-looking shoes, and they use bad leather."

"So how did you get here?" I asked.

"I walked."

"Walked? No! Arvo, that was miles. No wonder you're hurting."

"If it makes me free, it is the easiest walk I ever took."

"You look terrible! Medicine! I forgot to give you the rest." I pulled my backpack into my lap and got out the Tic Tac box with the last four pain pills I'd snuck from Mom's desk. "Here you go. You'd better hold on to them in case I forget again. I'm really sorry, Arvo."

He took the Tic Tac box, shook out a codeine, and swallowed it down. He closed his eyes and sighed like Mom does when she takes off her shoes after a double shift at the hospital.

"Do you really think the KGB is after you? You're just a translator," Giselle said.

Arvo rested his head back against the wall and kept his eyes closed. "I am a translator who knows that renegade officers are selling poison gas to Iraq. It is not a happy thing to know."

"Do you think the guy who got on the train could really be a spy?" I said. "He saw you struggling with your crutches and me helping, and he walked toward us like he wanted to talk to you." I stood up.

"He is older man with suit and bad shoes?"

"I didn't look at his shoes," I said. "Was it a black suit jacket with a black turtleneck underneath?"

Arvo nodded, looking very grim.

Giselle and Vivian stood up beside me and looked down the passageway that led to the back of the train.

"Arvo," I said, "I have a really bad feeling about that man."

"The KGB? Oh my gosh!" Vivian grabbed the gym bag we'd given Arvo the day before. "You have to hide!"

"You should disguise yourself," I said. I slid open the bathroom door. "Go in here. You can put on the shirt and tie we brought you." I gave him a nudge. "Go!"

Arvo hopped into the bathroom with his crutches. I dropped his gym bag on the floor beside him and shut the door. I heard Arvo lock it.

"Okay," Giselle said. "Let's get our instruments squared away while there's still space."

Across the aisle from the bathrooms was a long narrow room for oversize luggage. She slid open the door, and I could hear her rearranging the bags to make room for her cello.

"Here he comes!" Vivi said. She turned her back on the window to the car behind us and pulled me to face her. "Act natural," she whispered.

"Um," I said, racking my brain for a normal girl topic of conversation. "Do you think I should change my hair?" I looked over Vivian's shoulder. The spy guy was right at the end of the car behind us.

"Definitely," Vivian said. She pulled the elastic out of my hair and fluffed it up. "You've got to stop wearing a ponytail. It's such a grade-school look."

"Really?"

"Yeah, plus look! Curls! If you used some product and styled it, you would be really cute."

"Product?" I said. My voice made a squeak, because the spy guy slid open the door and walked into our compartment.

"Um, we're pretty much a baby-shampoo-only family," I said, forcing myself not to stare at the man in the black turtleneck. Something about him made my skin crawl.

The spy guy stopped and glanced around the compartment. He was not very big, shorter than Giselle for sure, and he had a long nose that was so bony and straight, you could slice bread with it.

"Baby shampoo, are you crazy?" Vivian went on. "You need curly-girl stuff. Really, Jody, we should shop."

The spy guy went into the other bathroom.

"Oh my gosh, do you think he's with the KGB?" Vivian whispered.

I held my breath, hoping Arvo would stay in the bathroom and not make any noise. Giselle came back out of the baggage room and grabbed our violins. As soon as she'd closed the door, the spy guy came out. I leaned toward the wall to let him pass, but Vivi leaned out at the last minute and bumped into him.

"Entschuldigen Sie, bitte," Vivian said, and the man said excuse me back in German, but he had a Russian accent. The spy guy looked in the window of the baggage room and then went on to the next car.

"Is he gone?" Giselle said, coming out of the baggage room.

I watched through the window in the door until the spy guy was completely out of sight and then said, "You can come out now."

"Coming," Arvo said, but it was five minutes later when he opened the door. Vivi and I just stared at him for a minute, because before we'd only seen him looking nearly dead or slightly homeless. He'd put on the blue shirt and tie and shaved all the hair off his head.

Giselle took one look at him and said, "Lord! Arvo, what have you done with your hair?"

"Is gone." He waved vaguely in the direction of the bathroom behind him.

"Wow," Vivian said. "You look totally different–like James Bond or something."

He smiled. "I have amazing escape car here in my bag– with rockets, yes? It unfolds. Is very top secret."

Vivian giggled, and I said, "There's more to you than we thought, isn't there?"

"The spy guy went that way," Vivian added, pointing to the front of the train, "and he was Russian for sure. What will happen if he comes back? Will he hurt you?"

"I will hide," Arvo said. "If this man is KGB–they are not gentle. You must not be seen with me again. If anyone asks you, Jody, who is this man you helped to catch the train? You must say, he is a stranger. I only helped him out of pity. They have no thought for children. When we come to Paris, get off the train by yourselves, and I will meet you under the big clock as before, yes?"

We agreed.

"Is this for packages?" he asked, pointing to the baggage room door.

"Yes. Come on." I held open the door, and Arvo followed me in. There was a narrow aisle and shelves along one side. "I'll clear a spot for you."

I walked to the back. Fortunately, the lamp had burned out, so it was plenty dark with only a little light coming in from the hallway window.

"Here you go," I said. "Sorry it's not very comfortable."

I straightened up to trade places, but there wasn't room to pass by Arvo in the aisle, and I could never decide if it was more embarrassing to squeeze past a boy facing toward him or facing away from him. I stood there feeling stupid. I leaned back as far as I could, crossed my arms in front of me, and looked down at my feet. Arvo was much taller than I'd realized. I barely came up to his shoulder, and he smelled like lemony soap. My hair caught on his shirt button as he brushed past. Just what I hated about my curly hair–it was always in the way. He started to untangle me. I brushed his hand away and did it myself, smoothing my hair down and tucking it behind my ears. He stood for a moment, his feet pointing at mine. Maybe he was going to say something, but I didn't look up to find out. Then he turned away, put his crutches on the upper shelf, and crawled into his hiding spot.

As I waited for him to get settled, every warning my mom had ever given me about talking to strangers ran through my head. Dad would freak if he knew I was travel-ing with a grown-up man he'd never met. Except Arvo didn't seem like a stranger. I'd thought about him constantly in the last three days and even dreamed about him. But when I forced myself to be logical, the truth was I didn't know any-thing about him–not even if he was telling the truth about why those men had tried to kill him. Dad always said I should trust my gut about people, but my gut couldn't make up its mind.

I looked for him or even a shadow of him at the back of the baggage room, but in the dim light from the door, he was invisible.

"Wow, it's like you disappeared. Good job." I turned to go, but then I turned back because it seemed wrong to leave him all by himself in the dark. And then I didn't know what to say, so I left.

Giselle and Vivian were already in the next car searching for seats. I looked for the spy guy, but he wasn't in that car or the next one, where we finally found seats together. By the time we'd stowed our backpacks in the overhead bins, given our tickets to the conductor, and showed him our passports, we had left the outskirts of Berlin behind, and the sun was setting behind the pine trees and open fields of Brandenburg.

There was an announcement that the dining car would close in an hour, so we filed back past Arvo's hiding place and into the dining car at the middle of the train. It had red vinyl booths like the soda shop on base, white tablecloths, napkins in a stand-up fold, and far more silverware than necessary, which was not like any restaurant I'd been to, not even the nice dining room at the enlisted men's club. I was going to order a schnitzel, because it's what I always order when my family goes out to a German restaurant as it's not very expensive. But Giselle ordered something fancy, and Vivian something even fancier, so I splurged and got the rouladen—meat rolled up in a spiral with a yummy filling. I'd only had it once before, on my birthday last year. It's my very favorite, and it didn't come with sauerkraut or red cabbage.

Giselle and Vivian were starting to get wound up about the competition. Vivian could never put up with less than perfection every time, and I was pretty sure winning was a big deal in Giselle's family. They were debating who was our toughest competition and whether we should have chosen a faster or flashier piece of music than Pachelbel's Canon to compete with. I chimed in a little bit, but my parents weren't like that at all. They always said, "Do your best," but they thought winning just came down to luck every time.

My mind kept wandering back to Arvo. I put all the dinner rolls and the butter packets in the top of my backpack, but I couldn't think of a way to carry some of my rouladen out of the dining car without making a huge mess, so I ate it all myself. Why hadn't I thought about food for him on the train? After dinner, Vivian treated us to kuchen and coffee with lots of cream. The coffee was just as awful as I thought it would be, even after three helpings of sugar, but the cake was divine, layers of chocolate and rum and cherries and cream with chocolate curls on top. We were just finishing when they shooed us out to close the dining car.

On the way back to our places, we passed the car where Arvo was hiding. "Catch up with you later," I said to the girls, and slid open the door.

"Arvo?" I whispered.

"Jody?" he whispered back.

I walked to the back of the baggage compartment and sat on my backpack across from his hiding place.

"Sorry," I said. "It's just bread."

"No, it is fine. Thank you," Arvo said. "I am not thanking you enough for clothes and food and money. What would have become of me if not for you?"

"You would have done it for me," I said. "If some American soldier was in trouble in your town, you would help him, right?"

"Rescue an American? I cannot imagine this. Americans never need to be rescued."

I asked him about his nights under the bridge, and he told me about watching the stars and the stray dog that visited him twice. He finished the bread and butter, and I wished I had more to give him.

"Are you still hungry?"

I could just make out his smile in the dim light. "Good company and plain bread is better than a feast all alone," he said. He brushed crumbs from his lap and shifted to a more comfortable position on the floor. "In the army I was always alone."

"It must have been lonely to be the only Estonian in your unit."

Arvo nodded.

"Didn't you have any friends at all?"

"Not one man I could trust."

"Wow. That would be hard."

I thought of myself next fall in a new school looking for someone to eat lunch with and not a single girl I could trust.

"I don't need a thousand friends," I said, more to myself than him. "I just need..." I pulled my knees up to my chest and rested my head on them, glad it was too dim for Arvo to read my face. I just needed to make time stop, so that I would never have to move away from Germany.

"You just need your quick-witted Vivian and your fearsome Giselle," Arvo said.

"Yeah. The army is moving us. After this weekend, I'll never see them again. When I was little, I didn't mind the moving so much."

"These friends are more dear?"

"Mm-hm." I bit at the corner of my lip. I was not going to cry. I hated crying.

"Musical friends are the very best kind," Arvo said.

"Musical friends?"

"When I was eight, I joined a choir in my town, an all-boy choir. That was very important to me at the time—no girls allowed." He chuckled quietly, and I had to smile thinking of him only a little older than my brothers.

"Later I did not mind the girls so much, but sometimes boys only is a very good thing. When I got homesick in the army, I sang to myself and in my thoughts I could hear my friends sing with me–Jüri and Jaan and Anton and little Mati, our tenor. I left my town and the choir seven years ago, but my friends' voices have never left me, even on my darkest day."

"Was it a church choir? I was in a church choir once." I was seven, so it must have been Missouri.

"No, people only go to church secretly in the Soviet Union. It was a town choir. Almost every town has one, for children and for adults, too. It is a very Estonian thing, to sing together."

"What did you sing?"

"The Young Pioneers made us sing all the patriotic Soviet songs." He sang a few lines of a song, sitting up straighter and moving his arms as if he were marching. I didn't speak a word of Russian, but I could tell it was a stupid song.

"Russian songs with no words are not so bad," he said. "Tchaikovsky and all those pretty ballet tunes, *The Nutcracker, Sleeping Beauty*–everyone likes those. But starting when I was your age, I learned songs in secret, songs in my own language." He put his hand over his heart and tapped a tempo with his fingertips, and then he began to sing a soft, slow song: *"Mu isamaa on minu arm."* He closed his eyes as he sang. The song came back to the same phrase many times.

"Gosh, that's pretty," I said when he'd finished. "What does it mean?"

"'Land of my fathers, land that I love.' It is the Estonian anthem. We have been forbidden to sing it for fifty years. A person could go to jail. Two years ago at our song festival grounds the audience sang it. There were three hundred thousand of us singing in our own language. My little sister wrote me about it. I've never heard her sound so excited—so proud of her country."

"Tell me about your sister."

Arvo reached into his pocket and took out a tattered photograph and handed it to me. It was well worn and the colors had all gone faintly orange. In the dim light from the door I could see that the girl was about ten and had the same nose and chin as Arvo. She wore one of those dresses that come with an apron that the German girls wear for Octoberfest. She wore a crown of daisies and cornflowers.

"Pretty. How old is she?"

"Eleven in this picture. She will be thirteen in a month."

I handed the picture back, and he put it in his pocket like it was a thousand dollars. My mom sent Aunt Cassandra new pictures of me and the boys every month. I had a whole bulletin board full of my favorite brother and cousin pictures. I couldn't imagine having only one picture of my own brothers.

"Does your sister have a choir? Does she have a good voice?"

"Last time I heard her sing, she still had a little-girl

voice—all chirp like a bird. She will grow into a strong voice if she practices."

"Practice makes your voice louder?" I said. "I thought some people were just naturally loud." I was totally thinking of Giselle.

Arvo laughed. "Being bigger helps, but a strong voice takes practice. How about you? Are you in a choir now?"

"Oh no, I can't sing!"

"Not sing? Bah! If you can breathe, you can sing."

"No, really, I'm not a singer. I'm a composer."

What on earth made me say that?

"A composer?" Arvo looked at me as if I'd just claimed I was a movie star. "Tell me what you write. Sing it."

"It doesn't have words. It's classical music. It's just the kind I know the best. I've got a lot to learn." Usually when adults asked about my music, they were done being interested when I told them it was classical music.

"I would love to hear something you have written. Will you play it at your competition tomorrow?"

"No, we're playing something traditional, Pachelbel's Canon, but the piece I wrote is a canon, too."

"Show me."

"Seriously?"

"Please."

I got off the backpack I'd been sitting on and took out my music notebook and the book light I used to read at night. I flipped through the first dozen pages to the opening measure of "Canon for Three Friends." We both scooted so we were sitting side by side with our backs against the wall.

"This is the part I play. The first violin for Vivian starts here." I flipped ahead a half dozen pages. "This is Giselle's cello part."

"Ah, cello," Arvo said, "the man's voice." He looked over Giselle's part, fiddling with the book light so that it fell on the page. "Tempo?"

I tapped my hand on my knee for moderato speed. Arvo listened for two measures and then he started to sing the cello part—just dum, dum, dah, dee, dum—but it sounded exactly like it had in my head when I wrote it. I had been nervous when I wrote the cello part, because I couldn't play the cello to check if my notes were correct. I closed my eyes to drink in the sound.

"Let's hear it together," Arvo said. "You sing the violin part."

"I can't sing."

"Everyone can sing. If you can breathe—"

"—you can sing. Right. Okay, I'll try."

"What is your starting note?"

I closed my eyes, because I had the violin part memorized. I hummed my opening note, and Arvo hummed his. The notes fit together perfectly. I knew they would, but knowing it and hearing it are not the same thing. Arvo tapped his foot to the same tempo I'd just given him and we began. At first I was thinking, I hope he likes it. I hope he says it's

good–I got distracted, and I was out of tune. But then I con-
centrated on my music, not just singing the right note, but
singing the note with the right feeling. By the time we were
all the way to the end, I didn't need him to tell me anything.
I knew.

9

Saturday, May 26, 1990
The Sorbonne

i woke up the next morning as the train slowed down on the outskirts of Paris. Vivian yawned and stretched in the window seat beside me, and Giselle got up mumbling something about a bathroom and a toothbrush. We got off at the Gare du Nord. Early-morning sun angled through the gray metal grid on the arched windows up by the ceiling. The lollipop-shaped lights were still lit on either side of the green columns that went the length of the station.

We headed toward the clock. I thought we'd have to wait for Arvo to get off the train, but he was there ahead of us, crutches tucked out of sight behind him, and a cap pulled low over his eyes. He didn't look up as we came, so we stood nearby but pretended we were not together. I looked around for the spy guy, but there were hundreds of people in the station even though it was early in the morning.

"We need to find the Métro, right?" I said.

"Yeah," Vivian said. "I looked at the map last night. We should take this red train to the Latin Quarter and get off at

Odéon and take the green line to Cluny, and then we are only three blocks from the Sorbonne."

"Can you walk that far?" I whispered. Arvo gave an almost imperceptible nod.

"I think we need bathrooms first," Vivian said. "To put on our recital clothes. I don't even know if there will be changing rooms at the university."

"Meet you at the Métro station," I whispered, and Arvo headed slowly in the direction of the subway.

Giselle and I trooped after Vivian down a flight of stairs to the bathroom and changed into the black skirts and white blouses we always wore for competitions. We put up our hair. Mom thought the outfits made us look like real professionals. I thought they made us look like penguins. We clip-clopped back up the stairs in our dress shoes and headed for the university.

Two Métro rides later, we were walking through the Latin Quarter. The streets were narrow but not crowded so early on a Saturday morning. Except for some construction workers and one well-dressed groggy couple who seemed to be heading home from a Friday-night party, we were alone. We came to the iron gate and then the carved wooden front doors of the Sorbonne. We followed signs for the music competition to a lobby full of people with name tags. We fell into line behind a quartet of older girls and a mixed trio about our age. The registration table was staffed by a girl who looked like she was in high school and an older woman who was deep in conversation with two other music teachers. We were safe, probably.

"Just sign Herr Müller's name where they show you," Vivi whispered to Arvo.

He signed the paper without looking up and inviting conversation. We got our program with the order of competition and followed the general tide of musicians down the hall and up two flights of stairs into an ancient lecture hall. Fancy plasterwork ringed the ceiling like frosting flowers around the edge of a wedding cake. The wooden floor was buffed to a honey-colored glow. The long wooden tables were pushed to the side and were so old, they probably had graffiti on them that said "Napoleon rocks!" Violin cases and sheets of music and backpacks and satchels were strewn about, and chairs were pulled up in groups as duos, trios, and quartets tuned and practiced their pieces.

I searched the room for an empty spot where we could have a little privacy to settle our nerves. A comfortably anonymous hum of voices in French, German, and Italian floated in the room, but then, a little louder than everyone else, I heard an unmistakably American voice. It was a flat, unmusical, middle-of-the-country voice. I turned around, and there was Mrs. Jorgenson and her string trio from Minneapolis, the trio that beat us in Frankfurt last year.

The kids were named Karl, Lazlo, and Megan, or maybe it was Maggie. There was no mistaking them; they were as pale as three puddles of milk. They looked like triplets with stick-straight pale hair and broad shoulders. I'd heard that they were farm kids from dairy towns in Minnesota and their parents had sent them to the music boarding school in Minneapolis. Vivi had carried on last year about how stuck-up they were because they didn't talk to her, but I could tell they were just shy. The girl smiled when she saw me, and I gave her a little wave.

Mrs. Jorgenson swooped over, all long black clothes and long black hair and dangly jewelry.

"Here you are," she said, extending her hand palm down to show her magenta fingernails. I couldn't make up my mind if she wanted me to shake her hand or not. Giselle glanced up from tuning her cello.

"The expatriates," Mrs. Jorgenson said with a very lipsticky smile. "We will have to be at our best to prevail today."

I hated being called an expatriate, like patriotism was bad or hopelessly old-fashioned. Plus I hated when I couldn't tell if what someone said was a compliment or a dig.

"How kind of you to say so," Giselle said. She stood up as she said it and shook Mrs. Jorgenson's hand. Giselle was taller than her, and she stood up good and straight to make a thing of it.

"Good luck," I said, trying to match Giselle's posture if I couldn't manage her height.

The boy from the Minnesota trio who was standing nearest me, the cute one with the square glasses, said, "Thanks, you too." He pulled a handful of Smarties out of his suit pocket and held them out to me. I smiled and shook my head. He was wearing a hand-me-down shirt and tie, I could tell, and he acted like an international music competition was nothing to get worked up about. It made me think we could be friends if we lived in the same country.

"And where is Herr Müller?" Mrs. Jorgenson said, still smiling.

The three of us froze. I turned to Arvo, trying to think of how I could possibly explain. He was gone. I glanced all around the room, but Arvo had vanished.

"He must have stepped outside for a moment," I said.

"He hasn't been feeling well lately," Vivi added.

"So I heard," Mrs. Jorgenson said. "I'll find him afterward. *Bonne chance.*" She turned back to her own trio.

Whew!

"I guess he decided to duck out of the room," Giselle said.

"We don't need him now that he signed us in," I said. "But weird that he just disappeared without saying anything."

I was disappointed. Now that I knew he loved music, I'd been hoping that he'd hear us play.

"Let's run through the beginning and then the last eight measures," Vivi said. We took our places and were just setting the tempo when the first measures of Pachelbel's Canon came floating across the room from the Minnesota trio's corner. All three of us stopped dead.

"They stole our song," Giselle said. We stared at them for an entire sixteen measures.

"We'll just have to play it better," Vivian said. We listened to the rest of the opening section. They sounded good—tone, rhythm, everything.

"We play right after them," I whispered. "Even if we play better, we'll sound like copycats."

"What can we do?" Vivian said with a shrug. "Play last year's piece?"

Last year's piece was good, but we'd lost to the Minnesota trio with it. We'd worked so hard to get to Paris. I wanted our song to be perfect. I wanted it to be ours.

"Wait." I took out my music notebook and flipped to my composition. "We can play this." I tore out the cello part, put it on Giselle's stand, and set the first violin part on Vivi's. "It's not hard. It's a canon, and it's about us."

"You wrote this?" Giselle said.

"Yeah."

"Jody, this is amazing. Is this what you've been doing all year on the train?"

"Yeah. Look, we're last. That means we've got more than an hour to practice. We can do this! The main theme is only twelve measures long, and it repeats a bunch of times. The bowing is not tricky at all. What do you think?"

Vivian was already going through her part, singing the melody line quietly, and Giselle was running her notes on the fingerboard without bowing.

"Oh yeah," Vivian said. "This is good." She read through to the end of the page. "This rocks!"

"Let me at it!" Giselle said, picking up her bow.

An hour and a half later we took the stage in the fanciest auditorium I'd ever seen in my life. It said SALLE CARDINAL RICHELIEU on the door, and it was breathtaking. The panel of three judges sat at a table directly in front of the stage, and an audience of a few dozen parents looked on. We were more nervous than we'd ever been. Giselle stood in front of us as Vivi and I took our places.

"Messieurs et mesdames," she said in her most polite command voice. "The Berlin American trio will have a change of program this morning. We will play the debut performance of 'Canon for Three Friends.'"

The judges looked at each other over the tops of their glasses.

"It's a composition by Jody Field." She flapped her hand at me to get me to stand. I looked from one judge to the next, wondering if we were even allowed to change our program in the middle of the competition.

The three of them looked very stern, but then one of them said, "Very well," in a British accent, and the old one said, *"Merci, mademoiselle,"* and gestured for me to sit down, and the one on the end actually smiled at me.

"You set the tempo," Giselle whispered.

I tapped my foot for a measure, and we counted silently for another measure and then we began. The room and the judges faded out of my mind. All I could hear was the sound of us playing.

The piece began shy and quiet, because that was how our friendship began when I was ten and even more shy than I am now, and also because when I started writing the song, I wasn't at all sure I could finish. The beginning was not my favorite part of the piece; there was nothing fancy about it, but I had to start somewhere. At least it was easy to play and followed all the rules of a canon. It gave us thirty-two bars to get over being nervous. Then came the main theme. We played it together with no harmony part because I wanted it to be like the first time we really listened to each other and the sound we made as a group. In the third part we had a musical argument. Vivi played the theme in double time, and then I played it at the regular tempo but with ornamentation, and then Giselle plucked out the theme on her cello and looked at us like we were so lame for arguing. I couldn't help smiling, because she really got what I was trying to say in the music. The last part was lots of long, strong cello notes: Giselle walking away from us in her long strides after our fight. Vivi and I played runs of scurrying notes, and now Vivi was smiling, because it was like us running to catch up with Giselle. In the very end we each took a turn playing the theme. Giselle's variation was very forte and strong to fit her take-charge personality, and Vivi's was dreamier, a thinking girl's variation. Mine was the bridge, like always. A little bit like Vivi's, a little bit like Giselle's.

Our last note died away, and there was a polite wave of clapping from other kids' parents. The three judges gave us a nod, and we left the stage. It wasn't a perfect performance. We were a bit off time on the fast part, but it was our own song, and I'd never felt closer to Giselle and Vivian than I did at that moment. I looked all around the room hoping that Arvo had snuck in to listen.

Mrs. Jorgenson was waiting at the bottom step. "Lovely. Well done. May I see your composition, Miss Field?"

I kind of hated to show her, because it was in pencil and it had a bunch of eraser marks and also ice cream smudges. I held it against my heart, but Mrs. Jorgenson just stood there with her hand out like I had to give it to her, so I did. She turned to the first violin part, and I saw her do all the things conductors do, waving her hand to the tempo and humming the notes quietly.

"Is this your first composition?"

"Not exactly. It's the first thing I've composed for trio and the longest one by far."

"It's a very competent piece—very balanced." She handed me a card with her name and the name of her school on it. "Please consider auditioning for a scholarship to our school. We are always looking for musicians who can compose."

That was exactly the kind of school I'd need if being a composer was ever going to become more than a dream. Dad would never let me live away from home, but it was nice to be invited.

The French judge took the stage to announce the winner. "*Mesdames et messieurs,* there has been a challenge under the rules of the competition. We will break for thirty minutes while we make a decision."

"What?" Vivi said. She turned to Mrs. Jorgenson. "Did you?"

She shook her head. "But I do think it will be a challenge to the use of an unpublished work, Miss Field." She looked at me in dead earnest. "Is this your original work and not a copy of some little-known piece of published music?"

"We saw her working on it every week on the train," Vivi said, scooting up shoulder to shoulder with me.

"Are you calling us cheaters?" Giselle gave Mrs. Jorgenson the look.

"You should write this on the bottom of every page," Mrs. Jorgenson said. She took a pen out of her purse and put a *c* with a circle around it plus my name and 1990 on the bottom of the first page. I took her pen and finished marking the violin parts. She found another pen, and I handed her the loose cello pages.

The British judge came over and said, "May I have a copy of your composition, please?"

"Absolutely," Mrs. Jorgenson said. She handed over my notebook without even asking me.

"Have you no other copy, miss?"

I shook my head, and he carried my notebook over to the judges' table with a frown.

I hated to leave my notebook with them, but I was exhausted from our night on the train and starved from our skipped breakfast. We trooped out of the auditorium and back to our stuff in the classroom.

"Hey, look!" Giselle said. "Lunch!"

Five croissants were set out on my violin case with a foil-wrapped cube of the soft kind of cheese. There was a paper package of sliced ham and a tall bottle of sparkling water beside Vivi's case, and next to the cello was a bunch of strawberries wrapped in the handkerchief that used to belong to Vivi's dad, and a big bar of the good kind of chocolate.

"Wow!" Vivi said. "It's like having room service. That Arvo, he's all right!"

"I wonder where he is," I said much more quietly. He wasn't anywhere in the room and wasn't in the hall, either. I went to look out the window. There was a steady stream of people walking down the street, but nobody with a blue shirt and tie and a bald head. I looked for the Russian with the black turtleneck, but all-black clothing was apparently the national uniform of France. Every fourth man wore it. I was about to turn away from the window when a man at a phone booth across the street turned around—black turtleneck, no hat, knife-sharp nose. Was it the Russian? I leaned my forehead against the cool glass. The window was old and had bubbles that blurred the view. Was I imagining things? I turned back to the girls and kept my worries to myself.

We ate the croissants first, prying them apart with our fingers and filling the middles with cheese and ham. It was so good, I could have eaten twelve of them. Fortunately, just one filled me up. We passed around the bottle of water.

"I wonder how much he paid for all of this," I said, feeling relaxed for the first time since we got on the train. "You don't think he stole it, do you?"

Giselle shrugged. "He must have borrowed money from us."

"I hope there's enough left for us to get youth hostel beds tonight." I tried to figure the price of the lunch, guessing from what it would cost at the market in Berlin. "Do you guys know the exchange rate for marks to francs?"

"One mark is three point thirty-six francs," Vivian said. Giselle just rolled her eyes like she did every time Vivi got mathematical on us.

Vivian brushed the crumbs off her fingers and unzipped her backpack. She pulled out a pink leather purse and sifted through the contents. She unzipped all the little outside pockets. "That's weird."

"What?"

"He still has my wallet. I wish he'd just taken cash. My passport and train ticket are in my wallet."

Giselle and I looked at each other and then at Vivian. I got a horrible feeling in the pit of my stomach. I opened my violin case and flipped up the lid of the rosin box. My wallet was there but the money was missing. I had stuffed my return train ticket and passport all the way to the bottom of the sheet music pocket on the outside of the case, but they were gone, too. Giselle dumped the contents of her bag into her lap and was unzipping the inner pocket. I could see a scream building up in Vivi, and Giselle looked ready to commit murder.

"He stole from us!" Vivi hissed. "I can't believe it. After all we did for him! We saved him!"

"He took all our money," I said. My mind raced back through the last twenty hours we'd spent together, looking for some hint that, what? That he hated us? That he was a rotten thief from the start? "And he didn't even say goodbye."

"We can't get home without the tickets and passports," Giselle said. "He's not far. Let's go!"

I set my violin in the case, snapped it shut, and slid the rest of the food into my backpack. Vivi and Giselle did the same. We had just turned to head out the door when Mrs. Jorgenson swooped over.

"Surely you aren't leaving without hearing the results? And where is Herr Müller? He will have something to say about this matter."

We stopped dead.

"We don't know where he is," Giselle said, putting on her intense and worried look. "Have you seen him?"

Mrs. Jorgenson looked confused. "No, is he feeling ill again?"

"I'm afraid so," I said, trying to copy Giselle's take-charge tone of voice. "I told him he should just stay at the youth hostel and rest, but he said he had to sign us in. Maybe he went back." Vivi nodded earnestly with a look of innocent concern.

"Oh, I see. That must be it," Mrs. Jorgenson said.

Maybe it was the concert clothes, because I've noticed people in uniforms automatically look like they know what they're doing.

"We should check on him," Giselle said.

"What hostel?" Mrs. Jorgenson asked.

"It's called the Young and Happy Youth Hostel," Vivi said. "It's the one that's three Métro stops away. We really must be going now." She turned and strode out of the room with Giselle and me right on her heels. We thundered down two flights of stairs and into the street.

The Latin Quarter

We took off across the courtyard in front of the Sorbonne and onto the Boulevard Saint Michel. We ran, not caring that people were staring, or even that we were crashing into some of them with our violin cases. Giselle's cello bumped along on wheels behind her. Medium-sized men in a shirt and tie were as common as litter, but men with crutches were nowhere to be found. In the window of an art supply shop, we saw a man who could be Arvo. We followed him down the street that led to the Panthéon, but he turned out to be a much older man.

It was crazy to think we could find him, but what could we do? He had all our money. We kept heading toward the nearest train station. He couldn't travel on a child's ticket, and no way would he want to go back to Berlin, but he could cash our tickets in for a ticket to Poland and be halfway home by midnight. But the farther we ran, the more I second-guessed myself. What if he caught a cab? Could he really walk all this way? And what was I thinking to travel with a stranger? He was a thief. What if everything he'd ever said to me was a lie? We finally made it to the Gare Montparnasse, but Arvo was nowhere to be found.

We were walking now, barely. We trudged through the Luxembourg Gardens and back onto the street. Across from the Odéon theater a beggar sitting on the pavement called out to us for money. He was young and handsome in a pirate way.

"Francs. Marks. Pounds," he said.

If I'd had a dime, I'd have given it to him. But I didn't. I shrugged and said, "Sorry."

"No!" he insisted. "Dollars! Pounds!" He grabbed Vivian's violin case and dragged her closer.

Vivian gasped as if he'd slapped her. I couldn't believe it; he'd touched her violin. People crowded right past as if this sort of thing was allowed.

"Let go! Let go! Let go!" Vivi's voice went higher with each shout until it was nothing but a mouse-sized squeak.

"Dollars!" the beggar insisted.

Even if her backpack had been full of bricks, Vivi wouldn't weigh eighty pounds. She slid toward the man. Her ballet flats had no traction on the pavement.

"Stop it!" I yelled.

I threw my arms around Vivi's waist and tugged her backward. Giselle squared her shoulders, tightened her grip on her cello, and got ready to kick the beggar's hand.

"Giselle, don't do it!"

I could picture her breaking his bones. I could picture us getting arrested for assault. I guess the beggar could picture the same thing, because he let go of Vivian's violin and spat out a long stream of French swears. We tumbled backward into the street. A teeny black car squealed right by our heels, horn blaring. The driver leaned out her window and yelled more curses at us. We stumbled across the street. Safe on the opposite street corner, Giselle and I sandwich-hugged Vivi until she stopped shaking. I didn't know what to say. It's not like we never heard swearing on an army base, but no one swore at wives and children—never.

"Where now?" Giselle said.

My mind was a total blank. I just started walking. I wasn't even looking for Arvo anymore. What on earth had made us think we could find him? Paris was huge, and he was just one person, one foreigner in a city full of them.

I was sweaty and there were red marks on my heels where Mom's black pumps rubbed. We turned right, down another narrow street crowded with little delivery trucks and the maddeningly delicious smells of sweet rolls and chocolate. Bike messengers with their cutoff jeans and long hair zipped by our elbows, calling out to us in singsong French as they passed. A few blocks on and there was an open paved square with a fountain in the middle and a very old church with a bell tower on each side and lots of columns in front.

We sat down on the pavement on the shady side of the fountain and rested against the yellow sandstone. A marble lion with a permanent snarl guarded us. Vivi kicked off her shoes. Sweaty red feet vividly set off her purple toenail polish. We sat there not looking at each other, and Paris was postcard perfect all around us.

Vivi said a swear. Then she said a whole long string of swears, and then she switched to German and French when she'd exhausted her supply of English cusswords. Giselle, who never swore because of home training, let out just one like a giant belch, and I said, "Amen."

"We are going to hell," Giselle said quietly, and with such conviction you would've thought she'd already bought a ticket.

"Honestly, Giselle, you are not going to hell for one little swear."

"We talked to a stranger—an enemy stranger. An enlisted man. I'm not even allowed to talk to enlisted men in our own army. My dad is never going to forgive me."

"We saved him," Vivi said, "and we took care of him, and nothing we did mattered."

I didn't care that he was an enemy, and I would have given him money if that was what he needed, but that last thing Vivi said had teeth. I didn't even matter enough for him to say goodbye.

"How could we have been so wrong about him?" I said.

"I can't believe he stole from us!" Giselle said. "He's a snake. He could have just taken the money, but no, he took our passports. Do you know how long it takes to get another? The forms? The lines? Mom hates the passport office!"

"I can't believe how grounded we are going to be," I said. "What are we going to tell our dads?" I tried to imagine calling Dad and asking him for money to come home. I wasn't even sure he had enough for another ticket. It was a big extravagant thing to send me here in the first place. All our other competitions had been close enough to drive.

"Let's not tell," Vivi said. She rested her elbows on her knees and fixed her gaze on the steeples across the square. "If we never tell them, it will be like it never happened."

"Oh please, Vivi," I said. "I haven't gotten away with that kind of logic since I was five years old." I twirled a strand of hair that had fallen out of my bun. "We can't just stay here forever. We have to tell them."

"No," Vivian insisted. "Do you remember the time in the fifth grade when I was pickpocketed on the S-Bahn on our way to lessons? I never told my parents. Mom would have made me go to music with her car and driver, and I would have felt like a total dork. Plus then it would have been just you two on the train together without me, and we wouldn't have become friends. I've never had friends who play music before. No way was I messing it up! It was only twenty marks, so I stopped eating lunch for two weeks and used my lunch money to replace what was stolen. Come on, girls! We can think our way out of this."

"Vivi," Giselle said, "this is not an algebra problem. It's not even a calculus problem. It's more of a lying-to-your-parents, helping-an-enemy-soldier-go-AWOL, and becoming-homeless-in-a-foreign-country problem. Where are we going to sleep tonight if we don't have any money?"

"But it's just money!" Vivi said. As if money was no big deal at all. "If we had money, none of this would be a problem. We could buy new tickets and hide on the train like Arvo did. He didn't need a passport to get into France. We can come home on Sunday just like they are expecting us to, and no one will worry."

Giselle pried up a loose corner of a cobblestone and tossed it across the city square. "So money is the only problem, huh? Great! We'll just knock over a bank and be done with it. You'll translate, yes?"

"We're going to start stealing now?" I squeaked. I could actually imagine Giselle doing this.

"Why stop at stealing?" Giselle said. "Let's hunt down that skunk Arvo and shoot him dead!"

"No!" I gasped, but Giselle and Vivian were already laughing.

"And then we'll join a criminal gang," Giselle went on.

"And then we'll overthrow a country!" Vivian added enthusiastically. "Just a small one; Liechtenstein would do, or Monaco."

"Definitely Monaco," Giselle said. "More fashionable. What do you think, Jody?"

"Umm, I think we need a plan," I said.

"A better plan than a life of crime?" Giselle said. She gave me a shove that rocked me sideways into Vivian. "Let's hear it."

"Well," I said, "we have a little bit of food." Because it's always good to start with something positive. "And it's not raining." Which was the only other good thing I could think of. I looked at the sky between the bell towers of Saint Sulpice and the buildings that ringed the square—not a cloud in sight. "And our parents aren't going to start worrying about us until Sunday night, when we don't show up at the train station. That's the main thing. They shouldn't worry. We'll get ourselves home and say we lost our passports. Our moms will be mad, but at least they won't think–"

"That we're pathological liars who went to a foreign country with a total stranger, enemy soldier, thief, horrible bad guy–"

"Right. That would be bad. Let's not tell them that."

"So all we need is twenty bucks each for the youth hostel tonight and forty-five for the train," Vivi said. "So that's a hundred and fourteen francs for a bed and two hundred fifty-five francs for the trip home."

"No, less." I took the train schedule out of my backpack. I hunted through the columns of prices for the right one. "It's thirty dollars because we only need one way."

"So we need fifty dollars apiece," Vivi said.

It might as well have been a thousand. It would take me months to make that much babysitting.

"So we could pawn some jewelry, right?" Giselle said. "Did you bring some?" She looked at Vivi, not me.

"No, they said no jewelry for the competition, so I didn't even think about bringing any," Vivian said.

I remembered the camera Aunt Cassandra had sent me, tucked away in the bottom of my backpack, and I didn't say a word because, besides my violin, it was the only fancy thing I owned.

"We could play," I said. "It's almost lunchtime. People will be sitting at those tables over there." I nodded in the direction of the Café de la Mairie on the south side of the square. "And there are plenty of people walking around."

"I could sit here," Giselle said, pointing to the edge that surrounded the fountain. "You two can stand. We know Pachelbel's Canon well enough to play from memory, and we've had the Minuet in G for ages. Let's see, Gavotte from the Suzuki book is fun and kind of peppy. Do you remember it?"

Vivi and I nodded.

"How about 'Für Elise'?" Vivian said. "Everybody recognizes that tune."

"I'm in," I said. We set my violin case open in front of us to collect money, and as we tuned, I had to lean in close to hear over the traffic and the splashing of the fountain. At least it would be hard for our audience to hear a mistake.

"So Minuet in G?" I said. I tapped out a measure with my foot, and we launched into it. It was a good song to warm us up. It had a lively tempo, and lots of people knew the tune. It had been our first competition piece two years ago in Hamburg.

Nobody stopped to listen. Some people tossed a few francs or a handful of centimes into my violin case without even breaking their stride across the square. A tour group passed by and listened, but none of them gave us money. We did the Gavotte next because it's nice and bouncy. People kept walking past. Most of them didn't even look at us, let alone leave money. We played through our whole repertoire three times. My hands got sweaty, and my feet were itchy and tired. I could feel myself getting a sunburn on my nose and the back of my neck.

We were in the middle of our third playing of Pachelbel's Canon when we saw a tour group of British girls about our age. They were in matching navy blazers, skirts, and knee socks, and they looked just as hot and uncomfortable as I felt. Giselle broke off from her part and started playing "London Bridge." The whole pack of schoolgirls stopped and looked at us. Their chaperone laughed, so Vivi and I switched to "London Bridge," playing it in a round.

One of the girls called out, "Hey, we're Aussies, mate!"

"Oops, sorry!" I said.

Giselle hardly missed a beat switching over to "Waltzing Matilda." The girls sent up a cheer like we were a soccer team and then began waltzing each other around the square or twirling separately or singing loudly and way off-key. I'd never played "Waltzing Matilda" before, but it's a catchy tune and not too hard to fake if you start on the right note. It was great to finally get a reaction to our music, even for something we weren't playing very well. Every single one of the girls came up and dropped something into my violin case. Sometimes it was a coin, but mostly it was penny candy. I didn't care. I could have hugged them all.

11

Along the Seine

As soon as the Australian girls left the square, Giselle slumped against the fountain and started massaging her left hand. I kicked off my shoes and stuck my feet, nylons and all, in the water. There was already a run in one leg and a hole in the toe. I was past caring. Vivian totaled up the money we'd earned. Not counting candy, it was almost a hundred francs— not even enough for one of us at the youth hostel.

"We're doomed," Vivian said. She packed up her violin and grabbed a handful of candy in white wrappers with green and red stripes. She tossed one to me and one to Giselle. "We'll be stuck here forever."

"Well," I said, looking at the extremely stern face of the medieval stone figure at the top of the fountain, "we could go to the USO or the American embassy and ask to call our parents. I think that's the whole point of having those places, right?" I unwrapped the candy and popped it into my mouth. It was tooth-crushingly sticky.

"Right," Vivian said. "I'm going to imagine that conversation now. 'Hi, Mom, it's me. I ran away to Paris with a stranger I met under a bridge. He's really old, too, like twenty-five or something, and a soldier, so I helped him desert from his army, and, oh, did I mention he's a Communist?' Yeah, that would go over great."

Giselle nodded earnestly. "Do you have any idea how much my dad would yell at me? He'd ground me until I was old enough to have grandchildren."

She was probably right about that. Dad said General Johnson never actually yelled, but he had this wrath-of-God voice that scared the heck out of people. Once when they were on a field exercise that went badly, Giselle's dad called in his intelligence officer and told him very quietly, but with lots of details, how inadequate his intelligence briefing had been. Dad said that the lieutenant's face turned gray, and he threw up right in the briefing room. I think I'd rather sleep out on the sidewalk than make General Johnson mad, and I bet Giselle would rather sleep in a pit of snakes than hear him yell.

I wasn't sure about my parents. I'd never done anything especially wrong before. I guess Dad would yell, and he'd probably ground me, too, but I didn't care about that so much. The thing was, Mom trusted me. She didn't dog me with rules or curfews or who I was allowed to hang out with. She just wanted me to tell her where I was and come home at a sensible hour. I would hate for her to think I was sneaky or stupid—that I trusted someone I shouldn't have.

"If we can just get home," Vivian said firmly, "we don't ever have to tell them a thing."

"Okay," I said. "We played for a little less than an hour, and we got about a hundred francs, and we need a little more than five hundred altogether, right? So we just need to play four or five more times, and then we'll have enough. We can play for five hours. How hard can that be?"

"What about the youth hostel?" Giselle said. "That's another hundred fourteen francs each."

"I don't know," I said. "I want to go home a lot more than I want to sleep in a bed tonight."

I took my feet out of the fountain and let them drip dry on the ledge in front of the stone lion. I looked at Giselle's cello case, with its engraved plate and built-in wheels. We could probably charter a jet home if she sold her cello. It was a hundred and fifty years old. But I couldn't even think about selling my violin, and I was totally not brave enough to ask Giselle to do it. Vivian wrapped her arms around her violin case and rested her head on the top. I bet she was thinking the same thing.

"We could look for a bridge to sleep under," I said. "Arvo slept under one for three whole days, and he was fine. The river is just a couple blocks away."

"Whatever we do, let's get out of these clothes," Giselle said. "We look like waiters."

We walked back to the train station and changed into jeans and comfy shoes in the bathroom. Vivian and I took our hair out of buns, and Giselle passed around the lip gloss. We headed back toward the Seine feeling much lighter and cooler and more peppy thanks to the candy the Australian girls had given us. I probably should have been more worried about being homeless, but honestly, it was hard to be gloomy in Paris on a sunny Saturday in the last week of May. Everywhere you looked there were little angels peeking at you from church rooftops and the smell of bread and coffee. France obviously didn't have that rule about a flower box in every window like Germany, but people did a lot more humming and kissing in Paris than they did in Berlin, that's for sure. Plus there was art around every corner. It's true that the sculptures were much more naked than they needed to be, but I didn't mind so much. There was never art of any kind on an army base.

By the time we got to the Seine, we were starving, so we sat by the water and got out the last two croissants and the strawberries. The bread was disappointingly flat after spending all afternoon in my backpack, but the strawberries I'd kept on top were divine. I couldn't help wondering why Arvo would steal from us and then go buy us lunch. It just didn't make sense. Wasn't he worried about getting caught? Or maybe he didn't want us to think he was a bad guy. But he could have at least left us the train tickets. The more I thought about it, the less sense it made.

I was hoping to see the Australian girls again, but they

wouldn't have recognized us out of our concert clothes. Lots of Japanese tourists walked by, and some Americans, probably college students. We saw a group of American MPs on the far bank of the river. It's hard to miss the armband that army policemen wear, and no one walks like an American soldier. Giselle and I immediately hid–she behind her cello case and I behind the paperback copy of *A Wizard of Earthsea* I'd stuck in my backpack to read on the train. They probably weren't soldiers who knew our dads, but we'd be in so much trouble if they were. Soldiers gossip like old hens.

By the time we'd finished eating, the shadows were long. Church bells chimed all out of phase with each other and in complete disagreement about the right number of rings. It could have been any time between two and seven o'clock. No wonder people in Paris never looked like they were in a rush.

"Come on, guys," I said, brushing crumbs off my lap. "We need to find a camping spot and then another spot to play music. Someplace with lots of traffic and cafés."

We gathered up our backpacks and instruments and started to walk down the sidewalk that went along the Seine. The first bridge had a smooth pale yellow stone arch very low over the water. There was only enough room underneath for the sidewalk, with no cozy camping spot up under the roadbed like you get with American bridges. We walked to the next bridge, and it was exactly the same, but this one had statues on top. The one after that was identical but with flowers all along the railing.

"Don't these people know how to make any other kind of bridge?" Giselle said, pulling her cello along to the fourth bridge in four blocks. "What do homeless people do around here?"

"Yeah," I said. "Maybe we could just find a bum and secretly follow him around and figure out where he sleeps."

"I bet they keep the bums pretty far from that," Vivian said, pointing across the river to the Cathedral of Notre Dame.

It looked exactly like all the posters, with square towers in front and spider-leg buttresses in the back. We turned south away from the river and headed back toward the Sorbonne because a university seemed like a logical place to look for bums. We turned onto a street called Saint Jacques. On the corner was a little green fountain with four cast-iron ladies holding up a basin of water. There were two trees with benches going all the way around the trunk and a bookstore with green windows and a sign that said SHAKESPEARE AND COMPANY in yellow and green letters.

"Hey, look, it's in English," Vivian said.

It's funny how your own language jumps out at you when you're in another country.

"Oh my gosh," Giselle said. "I've heard of this place."

"Me too," I said. "I think it was in the *Stars and Stripes* newspaper."

"This is perfect," Giselle whispered. "Come here quick!"

She tugged us around the corner. "It's an American book-shop, and it's run by this really old guy who's a little crazy. He has beds in the shop, and anyone can stay for free as long as they are a writer."

"Okay," I said. "That would be perfect—if we were writers."

"We're liars, aren't we?" Giselle said. "What's the difference?"

"Um, the lack of actual writing."

"Oh, come on, Jody," Giselle said. "Have some imagination. Everybody writes. You don't have to have a book."

"We're going to have to look older," Vivian said, already on board.

"Yeah, and let's write some books while we're at it. I'll just get started now."

"Don't be lame, Jody," Vivian said. "You write music, remember? 'Canon for Three Friends.'"

Giselle began to sing the cello line of my composition. Vivi chimed in with her violin part on the fourth measure. They remembered my music! And we'd only performed it once! I could have hugged them both.

"Okay," I said. "I'm in. So how do we look older?"

"We just have to fool an old guy, right?" Vivi said.

"No problem," Giselle said. "First, we can't all wear jeans. I'll change back into my skirt and blouse from the contest. Vivi, I think you should keep the T-shirt you have on, because it's nice-looking, and it doesn't have any words on it, but you should put your skirt back on. What are we going to do about Jody? Because we can't all wear the same black skirt, either."

"Definitely lose the ponytail," Vivian said. She looked at me with a critical eye. "I think if she puts on her white blouse and wears nice shoes with the jeans, she'll be fine."

"So where are we going to change?" Giselle said. "Because I am not lugging my cello all the way back to the train station to find a clean bathroom."

"There's a church over there," I said, pointing to a square steeple with a triangle roof on top. "It looks like it's just a block away. It's Saturday afternoon, so most churches will be open for confessions before evening Mass."

"Are you serious?" Giselle said. "We can just walk in and use the confessional?"

"Yeah, I guess. You just have to say some sins, and how hard will that be—lying, kidnapping, treason. I bet you'll be able to think of something. It's not scary, Giselle. I've been doing it since I was seven."

"Seven? Are you crazy?" Vivian said. "Seven-year-olds don't sin."

"You don't babysit very much, do you?"

"Well, I don't think I can go to confession. It's not my religion."

"Giselle," I said, reaching up to put my arm around her shoulder, "it's not about God. It's about clothes." I steered her down the street toward the steeple.

The sign outside the church said it was Saint Séverin. I guess the main thing with churches in Paris was to choose saints no one has ever heard of. Inside it was cool and quiet. There was a forest of stone columns that spread ribs across the ceiling like the branches of palm trees. There were chairs instead of pews in the middle of the church. We took our places on the right, beside the confessional doors. There were a few tourists walking around the edges and some grandmas with scarves tied over their hair sitting in the chairs. We watched the old ladies go in and out of the first confessional, but no one went into the second one.

"That one's empty," I said. "Watch the door for me."

I slid my violin under the chair and took my backpack in with me. It was dark inside the confessional except for a shaft of deep blue and amber light from the stained-glass window behind me. It was only a little bit bigger than a bathroom stall, with a kneeler, a dozen boxes of votive candles stacked in the corner, and a layer of dust on the armrest. I changed as quickly as I could without making any noise and slipped back outside.

Giselle went in, and I started praying out of habit. I asked forgiveness for changing in the confessional, just in case it was a sin, and then I confessed ahead of time about lying to the bookstore owner, but that didn't seem like much of a sin to me, either. Not compared to stealing from your friends—from someone who saved your life. I thought about Arvo lying on the ground spitting up river water, hiding under the bridge, all bruised and bloody, and sneaking around on the train because of the spy guy.

What if he was lying about his family in Estonia? Maybe he just hated the Soviet army and would say anything to get away. What if he was going to be all alone and homeless when we went back to Berlin? I bet he thought we were just another pack of rich Americans, even me. He probably thought it wasn't wrong to steal from rich people, like I think it's not wrong to lie for a good reason.

Giselle came out of the confessional in her black skirt and white blouse, and Vivian went in. I got up and walked around the edge of the church to look for a statue or window of Saint Cecilia, because she's the patron saint of musicians, but she wasn't in this church, so I went to the back where there was a nice statue of Jesus and Mary and a table with votive candles on it. I wanted to light one. I couldn't even say if I wanted to light it for me or for Arvo. But I didn't have any money to pay for the candle, so I just lit a match and held it up and watched it burn out in my hand. I closed my eyes, and I could see Arvo sitting beside me singing. I couldn't believe I'd showed him my music. Why had I trusted him? Was it just because he'd listened and acted like he cared? I'd never see him again.

I opened my eyes. There was Mary with a tender look on her face I hadn't noticed before, and then I had to look away because I suddenly wanted my mom. I wanted to sit on the sofa with her and her stupid-looking sweats and fluffy socks. I wanted to have cake with tea and talk, maybe not talk about this, but just talk. I wanted to be home.

Vivian came out of the confessional wearing her black skirt and pink T-shirt and sparkly belt. She did look older, maybe not like a grown-up but sixteen or seventeen at least. We went outside to the narrow alley on the left side of the church under a row of skinny-necked gargoyles, and Vivian took out her makeup case and got to work. I walked out of the alley fifteen minutes later feeling at least thirty years old. We went back up the Rue de la Bûcherie, and I tried to project myself as tall and fierce as Giselle and as pretty as Vivi. Thank goodness I wasn't doing this alone. We turned the corner to the bookshop. Vivi stopped me. She wet her hands in the green fountain and smoothed the flyaways in the French twist she'd done in my hair.

"Perfect," she said.

We pulled open the green door and walked into Shake-speare and Company. There was an ancient cash register on a counter to the right of the door and a table stacked with sale books to the left. Every wall was books from floor to ceiling. A shabby upholstered armchair was tucked into a corner. The middle-aged woman sitting in it had dozed off ten pages into a paperback that she held open on her lap. There were dozens of tourists with backpacks, and a man with a baby in a front carrier who rocked from side to side as he browsed vintage books. A tall man with a whole stack of gray hair and a big nose was moving books from a box on the floor to a shelf up by the ceiling. No one was standing at the cash register. Giselle started to look for the owner, but her cello kept bumping into people.

Vivian was about to go into the next room when the gray-haired man turned around and said, *"Mademoiselle, s'il vous plaît."* He set his books down and came over to us. *"Mesdemoiselles,"* he said, looking very annoyed.

"Oui, monsieur," Vivi said in her most diplomatic tone. "May we help you?"

"Now see here," he said smoothly, switching to no-accent English. "I did not book an orchestra. If you must bring an instrument into my bookshop, please make it a harmonica."

"You're Mr. Whitman, right?" Giselle said. "Well, Mr. Whitman, we're writers, and we need a place to stay tonight."

"Funny, you look a lot like musicians to me."

"We write music," I said. "Or at least I do." I could tell he was not impressed. "Writing music is still writing, isn't it?"

"Show me a composition."

"Oh." I looked at the floor. "My music notebook was sort of stolen this morning, and all of our money, otherwise we wouldn't be bothering you."

"Nice try, but I've heard this story before, earlier today, in fact. If you need help, call the police or visit the American consulate."

"I'm not lying. I am a composer. I'll show you."

I saw a stack of papers on the checkout counter

announcing a poetry reading. I turned one of the pages over and drew lines for music. As I wrote, Vivian explained that she was technically an illustrator, and did he want to look at her portfolio? Mr. Whitman began his no-thank-yous right away, but it took him three tries before Vivi agreed not to show him her drawings. Time enough for me to scribble out the first eight measures of my piece.

"I'm the one who writes novels," Giselle said firmly. "They are contemporary and very hip. They've got lots of sex and death in them."

"Ew!" Vivi turned to Giselle. "That's so gross!"

Giselle kicked her in the shins.

"Ow!"

"It's true," I said to cover up. "I especially like the, um, dead parts."

There was a pause, and Mr. Whitman gave us a you've-got-to-be-kidding-me look.

"Here's my composition," I said quickly, sliding it along the counter to him. "This is just eight bars of the intro, but I put all three parts down." Mr. Whitman picked up the page, and I could see him make the music in his head as he read through each part.

"Is there no viola part?"

"Well, no," Giselle said. "Because then it would be 'Canon for Four Friends.'"

"I can write a viola part for you," I said. "Do you play? If you let me and my friends stay here tonight, I'll do it."

"So you can compose just like that in one night? Are you so talented?" Mr. Whitman asked. He looked at me hard, and it's tricky to tell when a man's face is mostly eyebrows and wrinkles whether he's mad at you or not.

"I'm not so talented. I'm just going to work at it really hard and not give up until I get it right, because my friends need a place to stay, and the song is about being friends and sticking up for each other. . . ." I was going to say more, but I got a little choked up because Arvo ran out on me, but Giselle and Vivian never would.

12

Shakespeare and Company

"Oh, look, a kitty!" Vivian said.

A striped cat came in the front door and walked along the wall behind the sales counter. He jumped onto the counter and walked toward the sunlight that spilled in from the window. He made a circle of his body in the square patch of light and turned his face away from us.

"Kitty, kitty," Vivian crooned. She reached out to pet him. Vivi would cuddle a scorpion if it had fur.

"Do you like my cat?" Mr. Whitman said.

Vivian nodded. "What's his name?"

"William."

"William Shakespeare?" she said.

"Exactly."

Vivian stroked William's head lightly. He turned to her and snarled. There was a dark red stripe of blood on the side of his face from his ear down to the white patch on his chest that was the exact shape of Spain.

"Have you been playing with the neighbors?" Mr. Whitman said. He ran a hand along the cat's back. "Didn't I warn you about that?" His hand came away with blood and dirt on it. "A German girl took the apartment across the street. She calls her cats *Hans und Fritz,* but we call them the Huns!"

"Poor Will," I said. "Do you need a bath?"

Mr. Whitman wiped his hand on his baggy corduroy pants.

"If we give your cat a bath, can we stay the night, Mr. Whitman?" I said.

"Deal," he said briskly. "The bathroom is at the top of the stairs. Use a pot from the kitchen–third door to the right. Annalies will help if you need anything. You'll find her typing in the dining room–orange hair, soul of a poet. Welcome to Shakespeare and Company, girls." He gave a nod in the direction of the stairs and went back to his shelving.

"William, come on, William," Vivian said, picking the cat up around the middle. He hissed and scratched her arm and writhed out of her grasp.

"Let's try this," I said.

I took a faded denim shirt from the back of the chair by the cash register. I dropped it over William's back and swaddled him in it, claws and all, like he was a baby brother. I scooped him up, and he glared at me like he was thinking hard about what bribe he might give me to leave him alone. I decided not to use the word "bath" in his hearing. Vivi followed me up the stairs, carting my violin and backpack along with hers. Giselle turned her cello sideways and held it in front of her like a dance partner to get it up the narrow staircase. We walked down a dim hallway with rooms full of books on either side. Some of the rooms had couches or beds in them. One had a desk where someone was working, and the clack of a typewriter could be heard from down the hall. The bathroom was the size of a phone booth, with a prehistoric toilet and a sink not even big enough to bathe a gerbil.

"Right," Giselle said, surveying the miniature sink. "Brilliant idea, Jody. I'll just let you two animal lovers wash the cat. I'm going to find a place to put our stuff." She disappeared down the hall.

Vivi collected a pot, warm water, and dish soap from the kitchen. I shifted William to my left arm and opened the cabinet, thinking I could find a ratty towel that no one would mind if I used on the cat. They were all ratty towels. I took the one that was already gray and draped it over my shoulder. Vivi balanced the cooking pot on top of the sink and said, "Have you ever given a cat a bath before?"

I shook my head. "We had a gray kitten once, but Dad made us give it away before we moved to Germany."

"Yeah, me too. Mom always says we travel too much to have pets. Besides, they are constantly entertaining a zillion dignitaries. Pets would just get in the way."

"You hold him, and I'll get the soap."

I unwrapped William, and Vivi grabbed him around the

middle and held him over the water. She started to dip him in, back legs first. William curled his feet up and yowled like we were torturing him with boiling oil. He twisted his body around and climbed right up Vivian's arm and perched on her shoulder. He dug his front claws into the top of her head.

"Ow! Ow! Ow! Jody, make him stop!"

William glared at me with intense hatred and said bad cat swears to me in French. Sleeping on the sidewalk was starting to look inviting.

"Hey, sweet William," I said. "We aren't going to hurt you. Don't you want to be clean?"

William shared his views on personal hygiene.

"Oh man, you must be the new girls. I heard about you."

I spun around to see a woman with all-black clothes, a bright orange Mohawk, and a safety pin through her nose. A man with an Einstein haircut and a plaid flannel shirt stood behind her.

"You must have really pissed off the old man if he's making you wash the cat," she said.

"*Bonne chance,* ducklings," the man in plaid said, and he giggled as the two of them went downstairs.

"All right, Mr. Shakespeare," I said. "You are getting wet whether you like it or not."

I grabbed all the loose skin from his shoulders and the back of his neck. I lifted him straight up. Vivi gave a muffled squeak as his claws came free of her scalp and raked through her hair. I grabbed his back end with my other hand, lifted him off Vivian's shoulder, and began to lower him into the water.

William's legs immediately telescoped out to three times their normal length. He straddled the cooking pot and clung to the rim with all four paws. No wonder it took Mom an hour to give my brothers a bath. What is it with boys and soap?

"In you get, you silly cat," Vivi said. She pulled his back legs from the edge of the pot and lowered him into the water. William let out the most pathetic, you've-betrayed-me meow I've ever heard. I only put him halfway into the water and let him keep his front paws on the edge. Vivi scooped water up over William's shoulders and chest and front legs. In thirty seconds the water was black.

"Yuck! I don't think this poor cat has had a bath in a long time," I said.

Vivi squirted dish soap into her hands. She soaped him from shoulders to tail. I dunked him up and down a few times to rinse, but the water was so filthy, it was making him dirtier.

"We should get some clean water to rinse him," I said.

Vivian went to the kitchen, and I started thinking about how I was going to clean the blood off William's face.

"You must be one of the new girls," a man said right behind me, and I almost jumped out of my skin because I hadn't heard him walk up. The man was not very tall, but he

151

had lots of muscles. He was younger than the Einstein guy we met earlier, and better-looking, but he smelled like that stuff men put on their hair.

"Um, yes, how do you do?" I said.

I started to shake his hand because Dad always said a good handshake was as important as a good salute. But William squirmed away from me, so I plunged my hand back into the water and got hold of the cat.

"Sorry, very nice to meet you. I'm Jody."

"So what brings you to Paris, Jody?"

"Art," I said without even thinking. "I came to see the art museums. Umm, I'm a big fan of French art . . . and music, of course. I'll be playing with my trio at . . . a number of locations in town this weekend." Gee whiz, when did I get so good at lying? I guess it just takes practice.

"A writer *and* a musician," he said. He took a step closer and looked me up and down the way icky men did on the train. I would have pushed him away, but I was sure if I let go of William, we'd spend the next five hours looking for a wet, soapy cat in the bookstore. There were plenty of places to hide, I could tell.

"Will you and your friends be sleeping in the children's room?"

"We're not kids!" What was keeping Vivi with that water?

"It's the only empty room, and it has the children's books and a bunk bed. You'll have to double up."

"Oh, I see," I said.

"Come share with me. I don't mind doubling up. I'm in the poetry section downstairs."

"Excuse me!" Giselle said in exactly her father's wrath-of-God voice. "Thank you. For your gracious invitation." Icicles were not colder than her. "But no. We have other plans." Giselle stepped right into the creepy guy's personal space and looked down on the top of his head.

"Hey, what's going on?" Vivi walked up with a milk bottle full of water.

"The gentleman from the poetry section—" Giselle said.

"Was just leaving," I added as forcefully as I could.

"Okay, okay." He took a few steps back. "But stop by if you change your mind." He smiled and raised an eyebrow like he expected me to come chasing after him.

"Go!" we all shouted together.

I shuddered as he laughed, rounded the corner, and disappeared down the stairs.

"So. Creepy. Thanks, Giselle."

"No problem." Giselle shrugged it off like she did that sort of thing every day. "How's Will?"

I lifted William out of the water, and Vivi gave him a good rinse. With his fur all matted down, he looked more like a weasel than a cat. We rubbed him most of the way dry, which took three towels.

"Poor Will," Vivi said. She swaddled him up in a fourth

towel and hugged him to her chest while I got to work on the blood on his neck. He snarled at me twice, but I managed to get a look at the cut under his ear, and it wasn't very bad.

"Come on, I'll show you where we are staying," Giselle said.

We carried William along with us and followed her to the room with the children's books. A bunk bed was tucked into a corner beside a tiny window. There was a half-finished game of checkers on the floor and a blue-and-white toy chest where Giselle had stowed our backpacks. The instruments were under the bed. I sat on the bottom bunk, unwrapped the cat, and fluffed up his damp fur with my fingers. His coat, which had been dull black and brown stripes, was now a dozen shades of black and gray with a pumpkin-orange tummy.

"Aren't you a beautiful boy," I said, but he wasn't going to make up with me. He wouldn't even look at me.

"Now what do we do?" Vivian said. She passed around some of the penny candy. I wondered how long a person could live on Minties alone.

"We have to get back out there and earn some money," Giselle said. "How much more do we need?"

Vivian was totaling it up in her head when the woman with the orange Mohawk came to the door and said, "So, new girls, what's your game?" She had just enough of a German accent to trade her *w* for a *v*.

"Oh," I said, thinking back to what Mr. Whitman had

said about orange hair and the soul of a poet. "You must be Annalies."

"That's me–the keeper of the keys–so you better be home by midnight, or I'll lock you out." She crossed the room and sat on the bunk beside me. She reached out to stroke William's head, and he leapt into her lap, rubbed his head under her chin, and purred.

"Hey! He's orange on his tummy! I've never seen this cat so clean."

It's not that I liked William all that much, but it wasn't fair that I did all the cat work and she got all the cat love.

"So where are you from?" Annalies said.

The question stopped me; it always did. It's such a simple thing, and people ask it all the time, but when you grow up in the army, it's the hardest question in the world to answer. Should I say where I was born? Where my parents were from? The place I happened to live at the moment? I looked at the girls. Besides music, this was the one thing we shared. They both just shrugged. Say anything. Home doesn't matter. That's what they were thinking.

"We're from out of town," I said.

"And what are your plans?"

"Well, we need to earn some money, so we are going to play music on the street," I said.

"Okay. What kind do you play?"

"Classical mostly," Giselle said.

"That's a tough sell. Do you know any sacred music?"

"A few pieces."

"So go play in front of Notre Dame. It's packed with tourists, and when you see a group of Americans, play 'Amazing Grace.' You and your little angel faces, you'll make a thousand francs in two minutes."

"Really?"

"Oh yeah, Americans are ridiculously sentimental. Listen, don't stay in one spot more than an hour. Steer clear of the police. And if you can, try to play something a little bit hip–something your audience would recognize."

"Are you a musician?" I said.

Annalies smiled. "*Ja.* As far as Mr. Whitman is concerned, I'm a poet, but actually, it's all lyrics for my band."

"Hey! What kind of music do you play?"

The two-note wail of a French police siren drowned out her answer. I got to the window in time to see the taillights of three teeny police cars zip down the street toward the Sorbonne.

"Oh, what now?" Annalies said, exasperated. "If only Mr. Whitman believed in television as much as he believes in books, I'd have a clue about what's going on in the world."

"Is something bad happening?" Vivi said.

For a second I thought, It's Arvo! The police found him! But that was crazy. The police didn't even know that he stole from us. Nobody knew he was here.

"Down that way"–Annalies pointed south–"there are a lot of drug dealers, so I wouldn't hang out over there. Not after dark. But it could be terrorists, you never know. Everybody under the sun comes to Paris, and some of them are not nice at all."

"Dad did say something about Paris and terrorists a couple weeks ago," Giselle said. "Or maybe it was arms dealers."

"Things are kind of crazy these days," Vivian said. "The Soviet Union has always been so huge and strong and everything they did looked so permanent. Mom thinks that a year from now there won't even be a Soviet Union. Isn't that weird? Just Russia and a bunch of tiny countries no one has ever heard of."

"Well, I'm pretty sure that a year from now I'll still be grounded if I don't show up at the train station tomorrow," I said. "It's getting late. Let's go."

"Start with Notre Dame," Annalies said. "And you'll need to eat, too."

"I'm starving," Giselle said. "I bet we walked twenty miles today."

"You three look clean and tidy," Annalies said. "You could get away with the art gallery game. Plus with your instruments you'll automatically look serious."

"The art gallery game?"

I looked from Annalies to Giselle and Vivian, wondering if this was one of those things that would be obvious if you had a family that actually went to art galleries.

Annalies shook her head and smiled. "Babies. You really are new at this, aren't you?"

Giselle gave her the look for her baby remark, but fortunately, she wasn't paying attention.

"Every Saturday night there are gallery openings," Annalies went on. "It's where they start showing a new artist's work. There's a party with music and reviewers and all the artist's friends, but the main thing is there's food. Little snacks and wine usually. The snacks are tiny, but they have about a thousand calories each, so you only have to eat a few of them. Just don't hang over the platters and gobble them, or you'll get thrown out for sure."

"Thrown out?" Vivi said.

"Well, yeah, if they think you're vagrants, they'll throw you out, so don't act like you're starving. Look at the art first. Comment to some stranger about the sense of movement in the sculpture or the hopeful use of the color green in a painting."

"Okay," I said, feeling the urge to take notes. "Can any color be hopeful or just green?"

Annalies laughed. She was pretty, even with all the black eyeliner and the spiked-up hair. I bet she was only nineteen or twenty. "If the gallery owner is around, make sure you say something about the quality of the light. Gallery owners have a fanatical relationship with lightbulbs."

"Thanks," I said. "Let's get going."

"The gallery listings are in the newspaper," Annalies said, and then she disappeared down the hall. I grabbed my violin and my pocket map of Paris, and we headed out the door.

The Art Gallery

Notre Dame was a short walk from the bookstore, but the square in front of the church could have been another planet, it was so different from the narrow streets of the Latin Quarter. It was a football field in pavement. Enormous buses idled their smelly engines in a ring around the square. Groups of tourists clustered around guides or meandered on their own. It was hard to decide on a good place to play. We tried setting up in the middle, but nobody could hear us. I couldn't even hear us.

We moved to the church steps off to the left of the main door so Giselle had a place to sit and play. Vivi and I stood beside her, and the stone front of the church helped our sound go out to the square. Like before, almost everybody strolled right past us without looking–except for the kids. Kids always looked. The good thing about not having music stands was that we got to watch the people watching us. I could tell the musicians right away, because they stopped and thought about whether we were playing well. And they always gave a coin, but almost never more than one. Vivian kept a whispered tally of our profits after every single donation. I don't know how she kept track. No way could I add up change in the middle of a sonata.

Annalies was right about the power of "Amazing Grace" and a smile. We made a mint with that one every time. One group of old ladies in floral skirts and pink Nikes actually stopped and sang along in two-part harmony. It was kind of sweet. Giselle kept her eye on the time, and after an hour we stopped, even though we were making good money. I would have argued for staying longer, but I was starving and the sweet smell of a crepe cart was driving me crazy.

We were packing up when I saw two black sedans park behind the tour buses. Four men in black suits got out of each car. They didn't have the spy guy turtleneck on, but they had the spy guy look, and one of them had a radio. They spread out around the square and started talking to groups of people. I nudged Giselle and Vivian and pointed them out.

"What should we do?" Vivian whispered.

"Take cover," I said.

There was a group of tourists coming out of the church. Most of them were very tall. We grabbed our instruments and followed them, working our way to the middle of the group. We went with them to their tour bus at the edge of the square. It shielded us from the agents' view as we ran along the street to the Pont d'Arcole. I led the way across the Seine to the Right Bank and headed us north toward the gallery where there was an exhibition of a Spanish painter's work.

Just over the bridge was a big open square with a palace at one end that was straight out of Disneyland, only bigger. There were fountains on either side of the square and a carousel in the middle. Between the fountain and the front door of the Hôtel de Ville were a bunch of TV broadcast vans, a cluster of French policemen, and two men in American army uniforms. It was getting dark, and the TV crews were setting up lights. It looked like a press event–except for the black-suit guys with radios in their ears who were watching over the crowd in front of the camera. Maybe it was going to be a political speech. I was starving, so we kept to the edge of the square and avoided the crowds to move faster. Half a dozen police cars passed us going south toward the Latin Quarter. Maybe Annalies was right about the drug dealers down that way.

We headed north, away from the city hall. The street-lights came on and merchants were locking up the fancy shops. There was one just for handbags and another with all perfume and no makeup. Down the side streets I saw flower vendors closing up for the night and smelled a falafel stand.

"How much farther?" Giselle said, pulling her cello along more slowly now that we were passing a bakery. It's just no fair–whenever you're hungry, it's the good kind of cake in the bakery window.

"Almost there," I said.

Vivian looked up from counting change in her hand. "We made over a hundred and seven francs back there. We only need three hundred more."

"Just a couple more blocks," I said as cheerfully as I could, but I was totally thinking about breaking the window and making off with an entire cake–the chocolate one with raspberries on top. I got out my last piece of candy and sucked on it to make it last. We walked past the Picasso Museum and arrived at the gallery just as a bunch of ladies in suits and pointy shoes got out of a cab.

There were twinkly lights around the window and a sign with the artist's name: Isabella de la Torre. There was a fair crowd inside. We took a minute to check each other's hair. Vivian lent me more of her pink lipstick. We walked in, lured by the smell of something warm and spicy in the back room. I resolved to look at twenty paintings at least before devouring the food. The paintings were around the edge, and in the middle of the room was a cluster of pedestals. Each one had a porcelain doll on it in an elaborate vintage dress and tiny leather shoes. But in place of the china head was a skull of a small, fierce-looking animal. The artist had painted each skull with an elaborate design like a tattoo. I got a shiver looking at them.

"Wow," Vivian said. "I bet if the boys knew there were skulls in art, lots more of them would sign up for it at school."

Behind us, a slender woman in a sparkly black dress

laughed. "Let's not tell them then," she said in a Spanish-sounding accent. "So there will be more room for us girls in the art class."

I moved over so she could look with us. "It's creepy but cool, too. I keep expecting to see something in those eye sockets. It's hard to look away."

"If this was your work, would you put something in the eyes?" the woman in black asked.

"Could you stick a mirror down there, so you could see a little bit of yourself? That would be really neat."

The woman nodded and was about to say something when a man in a black suit and violet shirt and tie swooped over, saying, "Isabella, dear, someone for you to meet." And they walked away.

"Oh my gosh," I said. "I think that was the artist. I can't believe I told her how to make her art."

"She asked," Giselle said. "Don't worry about it."

"Let's eat," Vivi said.

"You two eat first," I said. "I'll catch up, so we don't look like we're crowding the table."

The girls headed for the trays of food at the back of the gallery. I'd expected everyone there to be like Giselle's and Vivian's parents, but I saw all kinds of people. Some wore fancy clothes, but others were dressed even more plainly than me. There was a young man in shabby shoes making sketches in a notebook. Another man had brought a little boy and girl with him, and he was having a very earnest conversation in French with them over by the skull-headed dolls. I immediately felt sorry for the dolls that lived at their house. I was sure they'd be decapitated by morning. I started working my way toward the refreshments when an enormous painting caught my eye. At first glance it looked like warm splashes of yellow, red, and orangy brown, with thin curving black lines. When I looked closer, I could see the outline of a girl twirling and splashing in water. The girl was not solid-looking, but wispy and light like she was a dancing flame. It was amazing. I couldn't stop looking at it.

"So what do you think?"

It was the artist again. "Um, well." I tried to think of what Annalies had said about colors and hopefulness, but I couldn't remember, so I blurted out, "I like these lightbulbs." What a stupid thing to say!

The artist laughed and said, "Yes, I like them, too." She pointed to the spotlight above the painting. "See, they put a yellow film over the light because this was painted outside in Spain in the fall, so you see the light must match for the proper effect."

I looked at the light and then turned around to look at the other lights in the gallery. "Hey! That one over the dolls is blue."

"I make the dolls indoors," Isabella said. "In the dark of winter."

"I can tell."

"You are an artist." Isabella nodded toward my violin case. "Do you find the music is different when you play outdoors?"

"Yeah," I said. "I played outside a lot today, and I learned that it's easier to make your music heard over the sound of water in a fountain than the sound of people talking. And I learned we sound best when there is a doorway behind us. I think the sound bounces out to people better."

"*Sí,*" the artist said enthusiastically. "Reflection is everything in art. Do you agree?"

She leaned a little closer and said, "Make sure you eat something before you play, or these vultures won't leave anything for you." The man in the violet shirt walked up, and she reached out both her hands to him. "Here you are!" she said. "I've met your musician—she is quite charming."

"This is not the musician," he said.

"No?"

"I have engaged the services of the Montoyo family—flamenco artists *magnifiques*! Unfortunately, not punctual. I deeply regret this."

"Oh," Isabella said. "But silence is not good for my paintings. What do you and your friends play?" She turned to me.

"This is ridiculous," the gallery owner said with a dismissive wave of his hand. "They are unproven. I have no references. Where are they from?"

"What do you play?" the artist asked again.

I straightened my shoulders and looked the gallery

owner in the eye like Giselle would. *"Monsieur,"* I said, copying the way Vivian would pronounce it, "we are music students." I decided that telling part of the truth was best. "You haven't heard of us because we are from Berlin. Our mentor is Herr Müller of the Berlin Philharmonic. We can't play an entire evening of classics, but we can play seven songs in popular classical repertoire. That's about a half hour of music. That would take care of your silence problem, right?" I turned to Isabella. "And a half hour is long enough for your other musicians to show up, or you could call someone else."

The gallery owner frowned, but I could tell he was thinking about it.

"We would charge only three hundred francs," I said firmly. "That's a fair price for all three of us, and we could be ready in two minutes. What do you think?"

Isabella smiled. She looked expectantly at the gallery owner.

"Agreed," he said, still frowning. He reached out and shook my hand.

Wow! I'd gotten us our first paying gig! I started grinning like an idiot. "Super! This is going to be so fun!" Then I remembered I was supposed to be a grown-up, so I added, "Miss Johnson will require a chair to play the cello, but Miss Armstrong and I will stand."

"Very well," the gallery owner said, and left.

I turned to Isabella and said, "Thank you so much.

You don't even know what it means to us to have a job tonight!"

She gave my arm a squeeze. "We artists must stick together," she said.

I gave her a little hug because I knew exactly what she meant. I was never going to walk past a street musician again without leaving a whole dollar. I skipped over to the snack table.

"Guess what, guys? We have a paying gig!" I grabbed a handful of the cheese pastry things and told Giselle and Vivi all the details. I totally talked with my mouth full.

"Oh my gosh!" Vivi said. "Three hundred francs? That's enough to get us home." She gave me a hopping-up-and-down hug.

Giselle hugged us both and lifted us an inch off the ground. "Jody, you're my hero!" she said.

"Come on!" I gulped down one more pastry and brushed off my hands. "I want to play better than we ever have so Isabella will sell lots of paintings."

We went to an alcove on one side of the gallery, where the owner had cleared some space and set up a chair. It was a different feeling to play indoors, for money, in front of people who probably knew a thing or two about classical music. I let go of all the things I was worried about: the money and Arvo and getting home. I put my whole heart into our playing. People didn't stop to listen in the gallery, which was just like the street. But I didn't mind. They weren't supposed to be *my* audience; they were supposed to be buying paintings. When I saw the gallery owner put a sold sign on one of Isabella's dolls, I felt as proud as a mom.

We were into our fifth song when a family of six walked in. There was a mom and dad, two kids, an uncle, and a grandma. They had a guitar and a violin with them, so I guessed they were the Montoyo family.

The gallery owner hustled over. "Where have you been?" he demanded in a quiet growl.

The man with the guitar shrugged and smiled. "We have been arriving."

"We did not engage a babysitter for your children," the gallery owner went on, still sounding angry.

"This is a family," the guitar man said mildly. "If you do not allow children to sing and dance with their parents, then my mother must perform for you alone." The man smiled kindly enough, but everyone else took a step closer to the grandma, even the little girl in the blue polka-dot dress. It was pretty clear nobody was going to mess with this family.

"Very well, you will play in five minutes," the gallery owner said. He walked away just as we came to the end of our piece.

"I'm sorry," I said to the guitar man. "I think he's grouchy with everybody."

"So long as the tiger pays me, he can growl all he likes," the guitar man said. "Please finish your set."

We ended with Pachelbel's Canon and played it better than we ever had before. If I'd known then that it was the last note we'd ever play together, I think I would have cried, but that night I was happy to pretend that this would be my future, playing concert halls and galleries all over Europe with my string trio—my best friends.

The Montoyo family came out and took the stage. They'd left their jackets and cases in the back room. The men wore white shirts with no tie, and the women wore red flowers in their hair and long full skirts. The gallery owner motioned for us to come to the back room. We followed him in, and he handed me three one-hundred-franc notes. I'd never held a bill with a hundred of any country's money before. I tucked them in my pocket and felt like a millionaire.

"Oh my gosh!" Giselle whispered as we went out. "We did it! We actually did it! I'm going to take all my vacations with you guys now. This is so much better than any Mom-and-Dad trip I've ever taken."

"Yes!" Vivi said. "We are rock stars!" She threw her head back and made a few twirls across the floor.

"Vivi, stop! You're going to break something." I grabbed her violin case before it knocked over the table with the art brochures. "Come on, let's find Isabella and tell her thanks."

I started across the room to find her, and the Montoyo family began to play. At first it was just the four adults clapping in rhythm. The grandmother and mom did a slower rhythm, and then the men did a fancier rhythm, one with claps and the other beating time on the tall wooden box he was sitting on. Then the mom switched to clapping double time, and the dad started to play guitar. After a while the mom joined in on violin. I was mesmerized. The tune was faster and more elaborate than anything I'd ever tried to play. I got so caught up in watching her fingering and bow work, I forgot all about Isabella.

The songs never quite ended but shifted from one to the next. After a few songs the uncle stood up and sang a solo. Then the boy got up and danced. At first I thought it was kind of mean to make a boy dance in front of strangers. My brothers loved it when I gave them twirls in the kitchen when we were listening to the radio, but they'd die if they thought anyone was watching. This boy looked like he was nine or ten. He was taller than Tyler and stick-skinny. He held his body very stiff and straight and drummed his heels on the wooden floor in time to the song. He never moved very far. The whole dance could have fit on your average coffee table, and he never smiled. Still, I could tell by the lift of his head and the way he was concentrating that he loved to dance like I loved to play. Watching him made me want to get out my violin and practice, practice, practice.

Giselle was into the music, too. She was tapping on her cello case in time to the clapping, and after a while she started to improvise her own rhythms. Vivian had danced the Spanish Coffee role in *The Nutcracker* last year, so she was doing a bit of her dance part with the little girl, who was only three or four. They twirled their skirts and took turns with the little girl's red and black silk fan. She taught Vivi how to move her hands for flamenco dance. Before we knew it, Isabella was shaking hands with people going out the door, and the caterers were putting away the empty trays.

"You girls are aficionados?" the grandmother said while the others were packing up their instruments. "You should come with us and hear what real flamenco music sounds like."

"Really?" I said. "Where?"

"Let's go!" Giselle said. "We don't have to be home until midnight."

"Bibi! Bibi!" The little girl tugged at Vivi's hand and looked up at her grandma, all big brown eyes.

The grandma smiled. "Did you make a friend?"

"Then we should feed them a better meal than this," the dad said, coming back with his guitar in hand. "This way, please."

We followed him out of the gallery and down a block to one of those tiny cars we'd seen zipping all over Paris. The uncle got in front and the little girl dragged Vivian into the backseat with the mom and grandma. I guessed that Giselle and I would follow in a different car, but then the dad popped open the trunk and the boy hopped in like this was a daily occurrence. I looked at Giselle and shrugged and followed the boy into the trunk, holding my violin in my lap. Meanwhile, the dad tied his guitar case to the rack on the roof and did the same with the cello.

"Lord help us!" Giselle muttered as she climbed in, gathering up her long legs and wedging herself between me and the side of the trunk. "We are all going to die in a wreck!"

I tried not to think about what my dad might say about all this—safety was very big with him. "We'll be fine," I said. "He's driving around his own family. I'm sure he'll be very careful."

The Café

The car sputtered twice. When it started up, it belched out as much diesel smoke as an entire convoy of Humvees. We lurched into traffic so fast, I would have popped out of the trunk completely if I hadn't been wedged in too tight for breathing. Since we were directly above the tailpipe, breathing probably wasn't a good idea. I glanced at the boy. He was calmly taking in the sights and not looking at me. He must have been shy. Giselle gritted her teeth. She had the edge of the trunk in a death grip. I tried to keep track of the streets so we could find our way back to the bookstore, but street signs were not well lit. And they were not on every street corner. And I realized that there was no comfortable position to sit on a tire iron. And I was beginning to think we were being taken to dinner in Spain.

But then we swerved onto a less busy street that was packed with taxis in every parking space on both sides. We putted along slowly. When a taxi driver got into his cab, the dad leaned out the driver's window and shouted something to him. The cabby waved his arm in a way that made me wonder if it was the French way to flip someone off, but then the uncle laughed and waved his arm in exactly the same way, right in front of his family, so maybe I was wrong about that. I resolved to do nothing at all with my arms until I figured out how not to flip someone off in French. Maybe they were just waving hello in Spanish. Hard to tell. The cabby left his parking space, and we took it. The boy jumped out of the trunk as soon as we stopped. My legs were kind of tingly from sitting on the tire iron, so I was way less graceful getting out of the car.

"Never. Again," Giselle muttered. "Where the heck are we? What if these people are kidnappers or something?"

The women slid out of the backseat, and the little girl was still holding Vivi's hand.

"They seem so nice, though," I said, leaning close so the others wouldn't hear. But then, Arvo had seemed nice, too. "Do you know where we are?"

"Don't be silly, you two," Vivian called over her shoulder as she followed the Montoyo family down the block. "Look, there's the Madeleine."

"And Miss Clavel?" Giselle said. "That's perfect, because I really think we need a nun right now."

I laughed, imagining the twelve little girls in two straight lines and their matching yellow hats trooping down the street to give us directions.

"Don't be a dork, Giselle. The Madeleine." Vivian pointed

down the street to a lit-up building that looked like a Greek temple. "It's a church. If we go toward it, the Seine is just a few blocks farther. We can walk east along the river until we get to the bookshop."

I relaxed, knowing the church would be on my map. Even if Vivian's directions were a little off, we'd be able to figure out the way back to Shakespeare and Company.

We walked a block to a tiny restaurant with green awnings in front and no sign of any kind on the door or in the window. It was like a secret restaurant, but apparently well-known, because the dining room was crammed with men in work clothes and great-smelling food. People turned to look at us as we went in, and every person there was either black like Giselle or brown like the Montoyo family. I wondered if they were going to be annoyed about Vivian and me, the way enlisted men are annoyed when a bunch of pip-squeak lieutenants turn up at their favorite bar on a Friday night. The grandma waved us to a table, and I felt better because there were some families with little kids nearby.

Everyone seemed to know the Montoyos, and when the mom and dad kissed the women working in the kitchen and then put on aprons, I figured it was a family business. There didn't seem to be a menu, just a long table with steaming-hot dishes. Grandma Montoyo showed us where to stash our instruments under the table. She handed us plates, and then she and Vivian had what sounded like an argument in

French. Afterward, Vivian smiled and said, *"Merci,"* and told us that it was the custom here for musicians to pay with a song.

"Okay." I looked around the room; it was not the usual classical music crowd. Most of them seemed to be cab-drivers. "What shall we play for them?"

"No idea," Giselle said. "We'll think of something."

The evening passed in a blur of food and music and dancing. I tried one of everything on the buffet since I didn't recognize a single dish. Most of it was fabulous, especially the thing with shrimp and sausage and yellow rice, but there was a fish dish with a sauce so spicy, I thought the skin was going to peel off my tongue. There didn't seem to be anything to drink but wine, and even though all three of us had finished the Just Say No class three weeks ago, we couldn't think of a way to say no to grown-ups that was polite in English or Spanish or French. We ended up pretending to sip the wine and making a bunch of trips to the bathroom to drink water from the sink.

Just as we were finishing our meals, some of the men pushed tables to the side and set up four chairs in a half circle facing the dining room. Talk died down immediately, and several of the diners went to the buffet table and took guitars and drums and fiddles from underneath.

Grandma Montoyo sang first. It was very different from what she sang at the gallery. Her voice was deeper and rougher. It was almost as much a wail as a song, but I could tell right away, even though I didn't speak one word of Spanish, that it was a song about tragic love. It was as if the ghost of her true love was standing across the room, and she was begging him to come back to her, and the other people were calling out to her to not give up, but no matter how much she sang, he could never come home.

I cried. Not that I'd ever had a tragic love or even a not-tragic love. I hadn't really looked for a true love. The quality of boy available in the eighth grade was not very inspiring, but for the first time I thought that someday it would be wonderful to be cherished so much that decades later he would still be singing about me.

After Grandma's song, other people got up and sang. One man brought out an accordion. Another one danced what looked like flamenco to me, but it was mostly feet and very little arms. A fiddler played and sang with a man who played a djembe. A man in a steel-gray turban played an instrument that was like a guitar but had a long neck and a pear-shaped body, and after that the grandma danced some flamenco with her grandson. Just as I was getting sleepy, Grandma Montoyo waved Giselle and Vivian and me over to take our places in the circle. I'd forgotten about playing music to pay for our supper.

"What would you like to hear?" Vivian asked.

"You delight us," she said. "Play something from your home."

Vivian and I went for our violins, but Giselle stood right

up in the middle of the circle and sang "Amazing Grace." Her voice was incredible–kind of low for a girl but powerful! She sang all five verses by heart. How could we have been friends all this time, and I never knew she could sing? I guess I knew she went to church, but I never thought about her singing in her church choir. When she got to the end of the last verse, she went straight back to the first and raised her hand for everyone to join her. I was shocked to see the entire room stand up. People sang out that verse, and they linked arms and swayed back and forth the way you see Germans do at soccer games. I didn't even think these people spoke English. Plenty of patriotic things have happened in my life–the army kind of makes a point of it–but I don't think I've ever felt so proud of my country as I did in that tiny Paris restaurant full of cabdrivers.

Vivian got her violin out and played "Simple Gifts," which is pretty even though it's a beginner's tune. Next she played a hoedown that got all the little kids up and dancing. I couldn't think what to do that would top that, but since the kids were all out on the floor, I decided to do some of my brothers' favorites. I knelt down so that the little ones could see my fingers, and I played "Pop Goes the Weasel," which always gets kids giggling when you pop the E string. There was a boy who was only about two, but he really wanted to touch my violin, so I invited him close and put my fiddle on his shoulder. I knelt right behind him and held up the fingerboard. I guided his hand with the bow, and we played

"Twinkle, Twinkle, Little Star" together. We got the best applause of the night.

It wasn't the first time I'd heard people clap, but before, it had always been an audience of parents. These people had no connection to me except the music, and I hadn't even played anything fancy, but there was something in that response that I wanted in my life. It was like the moment when you know you've found a friend.

The toddler scampered off to his mama, and I got up off the floor just as Vivi was saying, "Oh my gosh, it's eleven-thirty! We've got to leave right now if we're going to walk all the way back to the bookstore by midnight."

Giselle nodded, and I headed for the table where we'd left our violin cases.

"Bravo!" Mrs. Montoyo said. "You must come visit us again!" She touched her cheek to mine—not a kiss exactly, but so warm and friendly. "May we give you a ride home?"

"Why are you so kind?" I said. "We only just met a few hours ago, but you fed us dinner and now this."

"You love our music," Mrs. Montoyo said. "That is not nothing to us. And you made something beautiful for our children. Girls such as you do not walk through this door every day. Now tell us where to take you," she said as I packed up my violin. "You are students, yes?"

"Oh, right," I said. I'd forgotten hours ago that we were pretending to be grown-ups. She had been so kind; I hated to lie.

"We're music students from Berlin," I said. "We came to Paris for a music contest at the Sorbonne. I wish we lived close enough to come back, but the truth is we are moving back to the States in a few weeks. My dad is retiring from the army; I don't think I'll ever be in Paris again."

I looked around the café, drinking in the details. Of all the places I'd been on this crazy trip, this little restaurant, with its clutter of tables and faded wallpaper, was the place I wanted to remember most.

"Ah, the army," Mrs. Montoyo said. "You are American Gypsies then."

"Exactly." I laughed. I hadn't thought of it that way before.

"Good for you to have your music." She gave my hand a squeeze. "It is a thing . . ." She searched for a word in a language I'd know. "A thing large . . . but light to carry."

I gave her hand a squeeze back, thinking of Arvo carrying his boy choir songs into the Soviet army and all the way to East Germany.

"It's good for making friends," I said.

"Come, come," Mr. Montoyo interrupted us. "Here is your ride. Our friend will take you home."

The musician with the gray turban gave us all a very serious smile and said, "*Salaam,* young ladies. It is my custom to offer a special rate for fellow musicians."

"Let me guess," Giselle said. "A song?"

"If you please."

"Oh, I don't know," Vivi said, chewing at the corner of her lip. "I can't sing."

"Vivi," I said with a smile, "if you can breathe, you can sing."

Five minutes later, we were climbing into a taxi that smelled like pipe tobacco and cinnamon sticks. The driver put our instruments in the trunk, and we hugged all the Montoyos goodbye.

"Cinquième arrondissement, s'il vous plaît," Vivi said confidently as we settled in the backseat fumbling for nonexistent seat belts. Our cabdriver didn't have a request, so we sang every verse we could remember of "This Land Is Your Land," which only got us a dozen blocks. We made up new verses from our trip: "From the Latin Quarter to the Luxembourg Gardens," and everything else we could make fit the tune–Australian schoolgirls and black turtleneck spy guys. It was lots of fun.

We drove through a roundabout that had one of those tall skinny steeples with Egyptian writing on it, but no church of any kind was attached. The traffic got heavier as we came close to the river. When we finally got to the bridge, we could see a film crew shooting a movie and a very bored-looking policeman waving traffic over to a different bridge. We poked along with the rest of the traffic and finally crossed the river on a bridge I hadn't seen before. I was trying to concentrate on where we were, just in case, but the driver had turned on what must have been the news in Arabic, and I was yawning and rubbing my eyes by the time we stopped at the little fountain in front of Shakespeare and Company.

The front door was closed and the lights were off.

"No!" Vivian said. "What time is it? How can it be midnight already?"

I looked at the clock in the cab. It was 12:15. "Oh man, fifteen minutes!"

"Someone is awake," our cabdriver said. He pointed to the third window down from the door; a glow of lamplight came from inside. "There."

We piled out of the cab and peeked in the downstairs window. There was a lamp on a little table, and a sofa with a pillow and blanket on it, but I didn't see anyone in the room. The window was open an inch.

"Is this the poetry section?" I said. "Because I am not climbing in here if it is."

A voice came from inside. "Do you really hate poetry that much?" The Einstein guy stood up from a rocking chair in the corner.

"You have no idea!" Giselle said.

"Well, as luck would have it, this is the philosophy section."

"Thank heavens," Vivian said. "Can you please unlock the door, *please*? We were only a tiny bit late."

"No, I'm sorry, Annalies keeps the keys, and she is very particular."

"You've got to be kidding," Giselle said. "All of our stuff is in there."

"You look plenty spry to me," the Einstein guy said. He slid up the window and held out his hand.

The driver got out of the cab laughing and set our instruments on the sidewalk. "Crazy Americans," he said, and drove away.

"Come on, Vivi." I made a step with my hands. "I'll give you a boost."

She stepped up on my hand. After Vivian got in, we handed her our violins and the cello, and Giselle gave me a boost. Then she put her hands on the windowsill and jumped up high enough to haul herself in headfirst and land in a heap on the threadbare carpet. A cascade of thick and dusty philosophy books followed her to the floor.

"There now." The Einstein guy viewed the destruction of the philosophy room with some satisfaction. "Tell me that wasn't fun." He gave Giselle a hand up and then started picking up the books. "Wittgenstein hasn't had this much fun in decades, I guarantee," he said, brandishing a book with that name on it. "Nor Hegel. Now tiptoe upstairs, little ducklings, and don't worry about the troll from the poetry section. He met an untimely end earlier today."

"What happened?" I said. I picked up books from the floor and set them back on the shelf.

"George found out about the charming invitation you were offered this afternoon," he said, and then, noticing the looks we gave each other, he added, "George may look absentminded, but he knows about everything that happens in his shop."

"Everything?"

"Everything." He slid the window shut and placed the bar across to lock it. "There are only a few rules here. Make your bed in the morning. Read a book every day. And most importantly, writers deserve to be respected and cared for. When George heard what our resident poet had said to you, he hunted up a hardcover copy of *Lolita,* beat him over the head with it, and threw him out of the store."

"Wow!" Giselle said.

"You've got to be kidding! Mr. Whitman did that?" Vivian said. "He doesn't look sturdy enough to hit anyone."

"Doubt his sanity if you like—we all do. But don't doubt his strength or his faithfulness to his convictions." The Einstein guy straightened up the last of the spilled philosophy books and brushed the dust from his rumpled plaid shirt. "George is a remarkable man with a keen instinct for the best and the worst in human nature. Stay here just a little while, and he'll change you."

"We're leaving in the morning," Vivi said. She smiled, picked up her violin, and headed for the door. "So we'll have to settle for being changed just a little bit." We followed her out.

"Thank you," I said, turning back at the door. "It was very kind of you to wait up and let us in."

"It was no trouble," the philosophy man said a little wistfully, which made me wonder if he had daughters of his own somewhere.

We took off our shoes to tiptoe down the hall and up the stairs. I don't think I'd ever been more relieved to see a bed.

"We made it!" Giselle flung herself into the top bunk without even bothering with pajamas or a toothbrush.

"Hey, look," Vivian said. "Blank sheet music." She held up a sheaf of papers. "Oh man!" she said. "You promised Mr. Whitman you'd write something!"

"Oh, right. I remember." I took the pages from her. "You go ahead and sleep. I'll just get started."

Vivian kicked off her shoes, yawned, and was asleep in five minutes, hogging the whole pillow and way more than half the blanket. I didn't really mind. I was tired but too wound up to sleep.

I turned on the lamp that stood beside the armchair, went to the picture-book section, and pulled out a hardcover book that was big enough to be a lap desk. It was going to be tricky to write a viola part for my composition, especially since I didn't have the other parts to work from. I paced back and forth in the room singing the violin and cello parts quietly to myself and thinking of what the viola could add. I didn't have any brilliant ideas.

I tripped over a book on the floor as I was pacing from the chair to the window. It was *Alice's Adventures in Wonderland*. I flipped through a few pages, and the book fell open to chapter five. There was a stack of hundred-franc notes plus fifty American dollars. It made my hands tingle to hold that much money. Who on earth could have left so much in a book? A little parade of things I wanted ran through my head. I shut the money in the book and put it on the shelf. Those Gypsies who gave us dinner and shared music with us didn't have a lot, but I'd way rather be like them than like Arvo.

It was their music I couldn't get out of my head—the sadness of it and the power. I wanted to write something like that. There had been a bit of a melody in my mind all weekend that I'd thought of while we were riding the train. I pictured the Montoyo boy dancing in the rhythm of a train. I dug a pencil out of my backpack, sat in the armchair, and started to write a new song.

Sunday, May 27, 1990
Shakespeare and Company

The next morning I woke up still in the chair with pages of half-written music on the floor in front of me. It was hard to decide which felt worse, sleeping in a chair or not brushing my teeth. Giselle and Vivi were sound asleep in the bunk bed, still in last night's clothes. The sun was up, spilling light in through the dusty window.

"Oh my gosh!" I said. "What time is it? Vivian! Giselle! Wake up!"

I looked all around the room for a clock and then remembered that Vivian had a watch. She was still wearing it; quarter to seven, whew, plenty of time to catch our train. I gathered up the pages and set them on the windowsill, where Mr. Whitman would find them later.

Vivian and Giselle were not morning people. They growled and grumbled and pretended not to hear me. Annalies poked her head in the door and said, "Sunday! Free pancakes in the dining room in ten minutes."

That did the trick. Giselle and Vivi were up and dressed in a flash. Just a few of the bookstore residents were there. I heard snoring from one of the rooms along the hall. Mr. Whitman presided over the stove with a large bowl of extremely thin pancake batter that he ladled into a skillet and tossed in the air to flip. The pancakes were more sour than sourdough, and the syrup was watery. The only thing that tasted normal was the butter. If I hadn't been worried about hurting Mr. Whitman's feelings, I might have eaten a plate of butter for breakfast.

As people finished and walked out the door, Mr. Whitman called out various chores to be done around the bookshop. People grumbled as they went out, and sometimes they traded jobs in the hallway, but I heard someone scrubbing the bathroom and saw people walking past with brooms and dustpans, so housekeeping must have been part of the Sunday-morning drill.

When we had eaten as much of the pancakes as we could stand and cleared our places, I said, "Do you have a chore for us? Because we need to do it fast. We've got to catch the nine-o'clock train."

Mr. Whitman smiled and ate a pancake from the pan with his fingers. "You did your chore last night giving William a bath. I'd forgotten what a pleasure it is to have a clean cat." He put the stopper in the sink and started running hot water. "But I won't say no to some help with these dishes."

"No problem," Giselle said, turning up her sleeves.

"I'll get the table," said Vivian. She grabbed the dishrags from the counter and tossed one to me. "I wonder if anyone left a tip."

"Oh my gosh, that reminds me! I'll be right back," I said.

I went to the room where we'd slept and hunted for *Alice's Adventures in Wonderland*. I had been so groggy the night before, it was hard to remember where I'd put the book. Eventually I found it on a top shelf behind the door. The money was right where I'd left it.

"Mr. Whitman," I said when I returned, "this book was on the floor last night, and there's money in it." I opened to chapter five.

"What?" Giselle said, turning to look as she dried a dish. "Holy cow! That's hundreds of francs!"

"Twelve hundred francs and fifty dollars American," I said. "Do you think someone lost it?" I handed Mr. Whitman the bills.

"Twelve hundred francs? Really?" Vivian came and looked over my shoulder.

"It's not lost," Mr. Whitman said. "This bookstore is my bank." He extended his skinny arms and gestured toward the rest of the building. "When I have a little extra, I make a deposit. When I need a little more, I can usually find some."

"Are you crazy?" Vivian said. "Haven't you heard of interest? If you'd kept this in the bank for just three years, you'd have another hundred francs by now."

Apparently, for Vivi, it was never too early in the morning to do math.

Giselle shook her head, her eyes still on the money. "Anybody could walk in and steal it from you," she said.

Mr. Whitman folded his arms across his chest. "I find most people do not. And tell me this, Vivian. If I were to go to the bank and say, 'Please tell me the character of the young women who are staying in my shop,' will they tell me?"

"Well, no," Vivi said, a little flustered.

"You set that book out last night where I would find it!" I wasn't sure whether to be glad I'd passed his test or worried that he'd tried to trap me. What if we hadn't earned enough money to get home last night? What if we hadn't eaten? That money would have been really tempting.

"So, do you have enough money to get home?"

"Yeah," Vivian said. She turned to me with a smile. "Thanks to our genius booking agent."

"She's going to arrange all our tours of Europe from now on," Giselle said, laughing.

"Are you sure?" he said. He pulled out a hundred-franc note. "Do you need money for the Métro?"

"Wait a minute," I said. "You're just going to give us money?"

"Yes," said Mr. Whitman. "From each according to his ability, to each according to her need."

"I've heard of that," I said, remembering our talk under

the bridge with Arvo. It seemed like months ago and not four days.

"You are a student of Karl Marx?" Mr. Whitman looked impressed.

"Oh great!" Giselle said, smiling and shaking her head. "Another Communist! We've had trouble with you people before."

"You're a Communist?" Vivian said. "You own a business and everything."

Mr. Whitman smiled. "I'm sure in many records of the French FBI it says I'm a Communist. It might be more correct to say I'm a socialist."

"You do this all the time, not just for us?" I asked.

Mr. Whitman nodded.

"So that's why you fed fifteen people on three dollars' worth of ingredients, and there's a hole in your shoe?"

Mr. Whitman busied himself stacking up the clean plates. "Am I richer knowing you three are sleeping in the street? When our philosopher came up last night to tell me you had safely lighted upon his windowsill, cheerful, healthy, and unharmed, I felt like the richest man in Paris."

"So that's all there is to socialism? It's just being nice to people?" I said.

"Not entirely." Mr. Whitman smiled. "Would you like to borrow a book?"

"We are *so* going to be grounded if we come home socialists," Giselle said, and Vivian nodded earnestly.

Mr. Whitman laughed. "Off you go then," he said. "Don't miss that train."

"We won't," I said. "Promise." We went to the children's room, packed up our stuff, and made the beds. On the way down the stairs, I noticed a sign over a doorway that I hadn't seen before. It read BE NOT INHOSPITABLE TO STRANGERS LEST THEY BE ANGELS IN DISGUISE.

We headed for the Métro. It was a beautiful morning; the sights and sounds of Paris already felt like familiar friends. We walked down the Rue Dante with its little shops and brightly colored awnings and then turned onto the busier Boulevard Saint Germain. We walked past round kiosks with movie posters on them and newsstands with papers in dozens of languages. Across the street from the Cluny Museum, we went down the green staircase to the Métro station. The clock said quarter after eight, plenty of time to catch our train.

It was not very crowded on a Sunday morning. There were a few people who looked like college students and an older couple who were definitely American tourists, but there was also a family with kids, and they were staring straight at us and whispering. A businessman was staring, too, and then he went back up to the street. Just when I could feel the rush of air that comes in front of the train, there was the sound of men running and a command voice.

"You there! Stay where you are!"

We turned around to see two gendarmes thundering

down the stairs to the subway platform. A third was a few steps behind talking on his radio in rapid-fire French.

"Don't move!" the policeman shouted.

We bunched up together. It was the first time I'd ever seen Giselle look afraid.

"Vivian Armstrong? Jody Field? Giselle Johnson?" the officer said. "Are you alone?"

Three more policemen came down the stairs and stood in a semicircle behind us. Every one of them was huge and dead serious.

"Are you alone?" the first gendarme said again.

I was starting to feel very alone. I scooted even closer to Giselle and Vivi.

"No," I said. "We're together."

"You will come with us, please."

"No," I said. "We're going to the train station—the Gare du Nord. Our parents are expecting us in Berlin tonight, and they'll be worried if we aren't on that train." I looked from one disapproving face to another.

"You will come with us," the policeman said. "Is there no other person traveling with you?"

"It's just us," I said.

Vivi stretched herself as tall as she could, which was not very impressive at all, but she put on her most earnest voice and said, "My mother is acquainted with the American ambassador. You will please take us to the embassy immediately."

"Yes," the gendarme replied. "The embassy. Come this way, please." He gestured with his arm that we should walk in front of him up the stairs. We started moving, and the policemen formed a ring walking on all sides of us.

"Thanks, Vivi," I whispered, and I put my arm around her shoulder. We took the stairs together. Two police cars were blocking traffic on the street. Two more gendarmes were holding back foot traffic. Already there was a knot of pedestrians staring at us like we were criminals. We were hustled into a black sedan that was parked beside the Métro entrance. The driver didn't even look at us. Police cars drove in front and behind. They didn't run their sirens, but they drove very fast.

We were a tight fit in the backseat with our backpacks on the floor, our violins propped upright, and the cello across our laps. The policeman driving looked straight ahead, and the one in the passenger seat, who had done all the talking so far, said not one word to us in English or French.

"What on earth?" I began.

"They can't just arrest us," Giselle muttered under her breath. "We haven't done anything wrong. We have rights. Even in another country we have rights."

"But they know our names," I said. "How can they know our names?"

"It doesn't matter." Vivian gave Giselle's hand a squeeze. "Wherever they take us, they have to let us call our parents, and Mom knows everybody. Seriously, everybody. And she can speak French–diplomatic French and cussing French. Don't you worry."

But I did worry. Our parents knew. They must have figured out that we were in Paris alone. All our work to make sure they didn't worry about us was for nothing. I took Vivi's other hand and swallowed back the lump in my throat.

16

The Embassy

At the American embassy they brought us up from the underground parking garage into a room with a long meeting table in the middle. There was a smaller table with some phones along one wall and a window that looked out on a tidy green park and a busy street beyond. Vivian insisted we should speak to the ambassador, but the policeman said, "That won't be necessary," and left.

We set our instruments and backpacks down in a corner. Giselle paced the length of the room. Vivi eyed the bank of phones.

"Umm, so I guess there was a tiny flaw in our brilliant plan," I said, not looking at either of them.

"You mean the part of the plan where our parents find out anyway and involve whole police departments in foreign countries?" Giselle threw her hands up. "Yeah! That part needs a little work."

Vivian collapsed in a chair, took off her glasses, and buried her face in her hands. "We're doomed!"

I flopped down next to Vivi and kicked my heels against the chair legs. I couldn't think of a single good idea. Not one.

"I'm going to be dishonorably discharged from my family!" Giselle muttered, still pacing.

"And Mom's boss will find out and she'll lose her job!"

All I could think of was my mom waiting for me and worrying. What was she going to say to Kyle and Tyler when I didn't come home on the train?

We heard heavy footsteps in the hall. The door banged open.

"Jody!"

"Dad?" I stood up, my heart pounding so fast, I felt dizzy. "What are you doing here?"

My dad ran to me and scooped me up in a hug just like I was one of the little boys. He squeezed so hard, I could barely breathe. I could smell coffee and sweat.

"It's okay, Dad. I'm fine."

I could see Giselle's dad, who was almost a foot taller than Giselle, holding her face in his hands. He looked like he was going to cry. Vivi's mom was on the other side of them, hugging Vivi and stroking her hair. She looked just as suit-and-heels elegant as she had every other time I'd seen her, but this morning she looked hours beyond exhausted.

Dad pulled away and just looked at me. Before when I'd been in trouble, he'd always stomped out of the house and fixed the car first. After that I had to sit down and hear the list of twelve reasons why I'd made a terrible mistake and the details of every flaw in the planning and execution of my mission. But I could tell he hadn't thought of his list yet.

"What if I never found you?"

He whispered it—so much scarier than shouting.

"But, Daddy, I wasn't lost. I was on my way home . . . this morning. . . ." How could I possibly explain?

He swallowed back anger. "What if I never found you?"

The door opened again. I turned to see a silver-haired policeman with a very small mustache and a whole lot of medals on his jacket walk into the room. A young police-woman who carried a tape recorder and notebook followed him.

"Bonjour, mes amis," he said briskly. "I see the beloved daughters are returned. How very fortunate."

Dad switched to his soldier face right away, and General Johnson took three steps away from Giselle. Mrs. Armstrong tapped a manicured fingernail on Vivi's chest and gave her one of those we'll-get-back-to-this looks.

"You must be Mademoiselle Field?" the police chief said, turning to me.

"Yes, sir."

He came to my side, shook my hand warmly, and said, *"Enchanté."*

I glanced over his shoulder at Vivi, who mouthed *"Merci, monsieur"* to me. I gave that a try. He smiled at me, and then turned to Giselle and Vivian and did the same.

The police chief walked to the head of the table and gestured for the policewoman to sit beside him.

"Good morning, everyone. Shall we sit down?" he said. "I'm sure we are all very interested to hear how three schoolgirls managed to hide for nearly twenty-four hours from the entire Gendarmerie Nationale, a detachment of military policemen, and the diligence of ordinary Parisians who saw your faces on every television station in this city last night with a substantial reward for notifying the police of your location."

He paused while all three of us opened and shut our mouths several times without making any noise at all.

"I am prepared to be very entertained by your cleverness," he said, looking at each of us intently with half a smile. He gestured to the chairs again. "Messieurs? Madame? Mesdemoiselles?" We all sat down.

"Twenty-four hours?" Vivi said. She looked at her watch. "That can't possibly be right!" I could see her doing the math in her head.

"I don't get it," Giselle said. "We were supposed to come home today, and we *were* coming home. We had everything under control."

General Johnson leaned forward in his chair. "You were supposed to be with Herr Müller. You were supposed to stay at the youth hostel we agreed on. You weren't there!" His voice was headed straight for wrath-of-God territory.

"Mrs. Jorgenson called us," my dad said. "You didn't really think you could run away from the music competition and not have people care that you were gone, did you? Where did you go? Someone said he'd seen a man in a hat and gray T-shirt steal your money. Why didn't you just call us? For heaven's sake, Jody, I'm not a rich man, but I can afford to bring my own daughter home from Paris!"

"I didn't want you to worry," I said in a small voice. Not worrying them had seemed like a perfect reason yesterday.

"Who did you travel with?" Vivian's mom asked calmly. "Someone signed you into the competition—a bald man of average height, the witnesses agree." She looked at each of us in turn. "Where did you meet him?"

I squirmed in my seat, but Giselle and Vivian were staring right at me. I didn't even know where to begin.

"Did he hurt you in any way?" Mrs. Armstrong went on. "If it would make it easier to talk about, I will insist the men leave and this policewoman will take your testimony."

Vivi shuddered. "Mom! Eww! Of course not!"

Giselle folded her arms across her chest like she was the equal of any man who might cross her. "Hurt us? He was practically dead when we found him."

"Testimony?" I gulped. "Did we break a law?"

"Do you realize we thought you might have been kidnapped?" my dad said.

"But, Dad," I said, "why would anyone kidnap me?"

"Every military police unit in Europe has been on alert for the last eighteen hours looking for you," General Johnson said. "We interrupted soccer coverage on TV and radio to report your absence. You've been the subject of searches by the police forces of Germany, France, Belgium, and the Netherlands."

"It's me, isn't it?" Vivian said. "It's because you're–"

"An American diplomat? Yes," Vivian's mom said. "I know you hate the security team we have at the consulate, but extremists are growing bolder every year, and they don't care who they hurt. I should have been sending you to your music lesson with a security person all along."

"We were fine," Giselle insisted. "Nobody tried to kidnap us." She looked insulted at the very idea.

"I don't even understand how you got here so fast," Vivi said. "Did you drive all night long?"

"As you may have heard," the police chief said with a sly smile, "the American army has airplanes. We in France have found this helpful many times."

"You flew?" Giselle and I said together.

"A C-141," Dad said. "Emergency flight." He looked very grim. "We got in at six-thirty yesterday evening."

"Yesterday," I said. "You've been here since yesterday?" Pieces were falling into place: the American MPs walking along the Seine, the sirens headed for the Latin Quarter, the TV crews in front of the city hall.

"You took a C-141 for just the three of you?" Giselle asked, looking from my dad to hers in disbelief. "How? This isn't army business."

Dad told me once how much it cost to run one of those planes. It was thousands of dollars a flight.

"Just us *and* my aide," General Johnson said. "*And* Mrs. Armstrong's secretary *and* her press liaison *and* a representative of the German–"

"Yes, quite so," the police chief barged in, which I bet didn't happen to General Johnson all that often. "No bonbons for you girls, not one." He looked at us quite sternly. "I mean that, now. As for annoying Belgium and Germany, that's practically a national pastime. Well done! All that remains is to learn of your mysterious travel companion and the reason he brought you to Paris. Please. Enlighten us." He smiled, leaned back in his chair, and gestured for me to speak. The policewoman slid the recorder to my side of the table and turned it on.

I looked across the table at our parents. Each one of them was quietly furious. My mouth went dry.

"His name was Arvo," I began. "He was a Soviet soldier from East Berlin."

"A Soviet? What on earth!" Dad demanded. "What were you doing in East Berlin?"

The police chief turned to him with a polite smile, but Dad knew a command look when he saw one.

"He was a translator," I went on. "And he didn't bring us to Paris. We brought him."

I described how we went down to the river after our music class. I tried to concentrate on getting all the details right. When I got to the part about the attempted murder, Dad was ready to jump in again with questions, but the police chief held up a hand so he wouldn't interrupt me. After I told the part about pulling Arvo out of the water and doing CPR, I had to take a little break because I'd almost forgotten how scary it was to see a person look so gray and cold and then be alive after all.

"We have all heard of this cruelty in the Soviet armed forces," the police chief said while I was catching my breath. "There is a case in the German courts this month about whether a Soviet soldier is justified in his desertion. Such are the times."

"You saved a man's life," the policewoman said quietly. "You must be very proud." She turned to our parents. Whatever she saw in their faces, I bet it wasn't pride.

I went on with my explanation from the first day we met Arvo. How we'd brought him food and clothes. I described how we'd decided that our trip to Paris for the music competition would be the perfect way to get him safely out of East Berlin and give us a chance to play together one last time. When I got to the part about staying at the Shakespeare and Company bookstore, the police chief actually laughed.

"Whitman," he said. "Do you realize we looked for you in every hotel and train station in this city? And you found shelter with the one man in Paris who has looked after Americans here for decades."

"I can't believe we didn't think to look there," Vivian's mom said. "It's five blocks north of the university."

"Classic," General Johnson said. "If you want to hide, the best place is usually right under the nose of the person you're hiding from."

"We weren't hiding from you," I said. "If we'd known you were here, we would have saved everyone a lot of trouble."

"How could you not hear about the search when it was on every TV and radio station in Paris?" Dad asked.

"We were busy playing music, Dad, and bookstores don't have TV."

"And the end of the story?" the police chief said.

"Well, we played music on the street and earned enough money to get home," I said, deciding that the news of Gypsy cafés and climbing in windows could wait for some other day or possibly never.

Silence followed. I didn't even want to look at my dad. I glanced down the table instead. Giselle was slumped over and looked smaller than I'd ever seen her. Vivi had nibbled a spot on her lip to the point that it was bleeding.

The policewoman was flipping back through her notes. She raised her hand to ask a question. "This name, Arvo, it doesn't sound Russian. Did he not tell you his last name?"

"Kross," I said. "Arvo Kross, and he's not Russian; he's Estonian. He hates the Soviet Union. He wants to go home to Estonia. He wants his country to be free."

"Sergeant Kross," General Johnson said very quietly. "I'll be damned. He's alive."

17

The Embassy

GENERAL Johnson and my dad exchanged a look. I knew that look. It was the one Dad always got right before the base went on an alert and he worked around the clock for days on end.

They both stood up, and General Johnson said, "I believe we have people to call." He motioned the police chief and Mrs. Armstrong to the side of the room by the phones. They had a very intense conversation in whispers.

My stomach was starting to growl. The disgusting pancakes we ate seemed like hours ago. Our penny candy was long gone.

The police chief returned to the conference table where the three of us were still sitting and said, "We will need to secure your bags as evidence."

"Evidence?" I said. Dad had finished his conversation with the others and was headed my way. "Evidence of what?"

Giselle scooted her chair closer to mine. "We get it that it was wrong to lie to our parents, but that's not a crime, is it?"

"Jody," Dad said, "do you remember last Tuesday? It was the night you found Sergeant Kross. I came home late that night."

"Yeah," I said. "We talked about houses and moving to Texas."

"The base was on alert because the day before, we'd received information about—well, never mind what it was about—dangerous information from a Soviet informant. We had a plan to intercept something and retrieve our informant."

"I know, Dad. Arvo told us. They were going to make him carry poison gas to sell in Iraq, or maybe it was Iran, one of those places."

"Iraq," Dad said quietly but firmly. General Johnson nodded, and they both looked terribly serious—not just serious but heavy, worried.

"Someone betrayed him, Dad. His officers found out that he went to you for help, and they beat him up. It's why they threw him off the bridge. He said a spy turned him in."

"More likely someone listened on his phone," Dad said. "Eavesdropping is big business in East Germany." He shook his head and ran a hand over his close-cropped hair. "We almost had him. If we'd gotten there a few hours sooner, he'd have been safe."

"But what about his family?" I said. "We tried to get him to come back to the base with us, but he wouldn't because he was afraid they'd arrest his mom and his sister. He was so worried about them."

Dad shook his head. "If they think Sergeant Kross died on that bridge, then there is no reason for them to harass his family. Don't you worry about them."

"I'm not sure they believe he died. I think Arvo was followed here to Paris."

"Followed?"

"Well, there was a guy, a Russian guy, who followed us onto the train, and I saw him again when we were at the music competition." I looked from my dad to the chief of police, who gave me an encouraging nod. "There were some men in suits in front of Notre Dame last night, right before it got dark, and they were looking for someone."

"So let's assume we are not the only ones looking for the elusive Sergeant Kross," the French police chief said. He got to work on the phones.

Eventually someone brought in lunches, our bags were searched, and we were questioned at length by an American and a British man whose jobs were never exactly explained, but I could guess. They kept coming back to the question of whether or not Arvo had given us something to carry or asked us to call someone or to meet him later. My patience for repeating myself was wearing thin. At last the British man stood up and walked over to the other table to get tea. I followed him, even though I'd already drunk three cups.

"So, Jody," he said in a less businesslike voice than before. "What sort of a man is this Arvo? Do you like him?" He poured the tea.

Dad had stepped out of the room, and everyone else was busy.

"Yes," I said quietly. "I liked him very much. He listened to me. I told him I want to be a composer, and he sang with me. That's what Estonians do. They sing. And he acted like being a composer was a thing an ordinary person could do—a thing I could do. Plus I thought he was dead when I first pulled him out of the river, but he wasn't, and I can't stop thinking about him and wondering if he's okay. Yesterday, when we were walking on a bridge over the Seine, I couldn't help looking for him in the water. It's crazy." I poured milk and sugar into my tea. "He stole from us."

The British agent looked over the tray of cookies. "You saved his life. That makes this different from any other friendship you've had."

"It can't be much of a friendship if he stole our money and our tickets and our passports. If he'd just asked, I'd have given him money."

"Curious that he stole your money and then bought you lunch. That doesn't exactly sound like the action of an enemy."

The American agent strolled over, grabbed the last handful of cookies, and started fiddling with the coffeepot. "I've been thinking about that lunch, too," he said, popping a cookie into his mouth. He had an accent I remembered from my kindergarten teacher, so it must have been a Texas accent. "You'd think he'd be in a bigger hurry to run."

"Did you say he could find a friend in Paris?" the British agent asked. "Did he have someone specific in mind?"

"No, we decided to find some escaped Estonians living in Paris. We were going to start by finding a Lutheran church."

"Well, Miss Jody," the Texan said, "that was a good plan. Any Lutheran pastor you could have found would have been the logical and law-abiding type. He'd have called your parents and straightened this whole thing out."

"So Arvo's not in trouble?" I said. "I mean, when you find him, you aren't going to make him go back to his unit in Berlin, are you?"

The British agent smiled. "No. Mind you, we'll speak to him about stealing from children, but he did mean to help us. He has information we need about the flow of weapons out of the Soviet Union. He's far too valuable for us to just let him go."

"We did try to rescue him," the agent from Texas added. "We just didn't get there in time. You, on the other hand, were able to accomplish what your father and one of the most highly respected generals in all of Europe were not, not with twenty years of experience in military operations and all the resources that come along with two stars on your hat."

My mouth fell right open. "Seriously?"

"Oh yes. They spent the last hour on the phone explaining to the Supreme Allied Commander in Europe how three schoolgirls saved the life of their Soviet contact. Not a happy conversation for them, I imagine."

"We'll never see that man again." The British agent drank down the last of his tea. "Soviets are a paranoid lot. He'll never stop running."

"Well, he can't exactly run," I said. "He can barely walk."

"What?" both the agents said together.

"He broke his leg, remember?" But then I couldn't remember myself, after all those questions, if I had mentioned the broken ankle, and then I realized I had glossed over that part because I didn't want to say, in front of Dad, that I'd stolen the painkillers from our house.

"He broke his ankle," I said. "It was all puffy and pointed in a wrong direction when I first got him out of the water. So when I brought food, I also brought some Tylenol with codeine."

I looked from one to the other, but neither of them seemed especially shocked. I guess everyone knew soldiers took that stuff for training injuries all the time.

"Arvo managed to splint his broken ankle himself, but he was in terrible shape. The pain medicine helped. Except it ran out by Friday, and he almost fainted when we had to run to catch the train. He went all gray and sweaty. But he didn't give up. Not even after the spy guy followed us onto the train."

I shivered, remembering what Arvo had said about the KGB having no mercy, not even for children. I thought about him sitting on the baggage-room floor all night not knowing if the agent would catch him there. I bet he didn't sleep for one minute. And after all that, he still went out and got us food. Could they have seen each other in the market? Did he know the KGB was just outside the university?

"I think I can guess where Arvo is," I said slowly. "What if he never left the Sorbonne after he got us lunch? What if he stayed put? General Johnson was just saying that right under our noses is a good place to hide. Plus the army manual says if you are shot down and injured, you should hide and heal before you try to run—at least the American one does."

"How extraordinary," the British agent said. "The Sorbonne is full of empty spaces, and Sergeant Kross is the right age to be mistaken for a student. A certain amount of scruffiness that would call attention elsewhere would hardly generate notice among college students."

"It would take us ages to search the place," the American agent added. "I suppose eventually he'll need food."

"Eventually he'll need pain medicine," I said. "He took one when we got on the train, and then I gave him three more because that was all that was left at home. So that's . . ." I counted doses twelve hours apart. "He'll be wanting more pain medicine by six o'clock tonight. Maybe if you looked for him at emergency rooms or wherever it is French people go for medicine, you'll find him."

"Brilliant!" the British agent said, and he reached into his pocket and handed me his business card. "If you find music not to your liking, I hope you'll consider intelligence work. You've already got as much courage and savvy as half the people I work with."

The Eiffel Tower

"Gentlemen," the British agent said, turning to the other men in the room, "we have a solid lead, and if we can turn out enough men on the street, I think we can find Sergeant Kross in the next few hours." He explained where he thought Arvo was and how to find him.

Giselle, Vivian, and I were left at the table, suddenly unimportant. I couldn't decide if I wanted to see Arvo again or not. I couldn't even decide if I was mad at him for stealing our money. Maybe learning that I could take care of myself in a foreign city was worth it. Vivian took a deck of cards out of her pocket and started up a game of spoons, but I wasn't really into it.

About an hour later our parents came back in, with the French police chief right behind them.

"Good news," Mrs. Armstrong called out.

The police chief strode up to the table. "Sergeant Kross has been recovered, hungry but alive," he said.

I let out a huge breath I didn't even realize I'd been holding.

"And our friends in the KGB," the police chief went on, "are now following the wrong man on a chase that will be as difficult and costly as we can possibly make it."

General Johnson nodded in admiration. "Those boys are in for a cold day in Moscow if they ever make it home."

"They'll see a cold day before the Palace of Justice if they break even one law on French soil," the police chief said, with no trace of his usual charm.

"Where is Arvo now?" I said.

"On a helicopter to the hospital at Ramstein Air Base," General Johnson said. "He'll need X-rays and a cast, and also a quiet and safe place to work with the brigade intelligence officer and others sorting out what he knows about weapons transport."

"However," the police chief said, "he insisted you have this immediately." He handed us a large envelope with a flourish. I opened it, and out slid a stack of cash, three passports, and a set of second-class train tickets.

"He was very concerned about these girls," the police chief said to our parents. "He didn't want the Soviet agent to see all of them together and bring them to harm. He thought if he took their passports and money, they'd go to the embassy for help immediately."

The police chief turned to the three of us with a stern look. "He was right, mesdemoiselles. They would have helped you at the embassy. Any gendarme on the street, probably any citizen of Paris, would have helped you, if only you had asked." He paused while the weight of that sank in. It was true. Everyone we'd met had been kind.

"Next time you visit my city, you will not be so shy–or perhaps not so spirited. Do you promise?"

"Yes, sir," we each said in turn.

"So all is mended then?" the British agent said. "Well done!" He stood up, and the American agent with him. "We have reports to file. You will remember what I said, Miss Field?"

I nodded and waved as the two left the room. The police chief followed them out, and then it was just us and our parents alone in the conference room.

For a moment no one said anything. Dad peered into his empty coffee cup. Vivi's mom put her feet up on a chair. General Johnson actually took off the tie on his Class A uniform. They all looked exactly like people who hadn't slept in two days.

"Dad, I'm sorry–" I began.

He shook his head. "Do you have any idea how worried people have been about you? The number of people? The hours?"

"We were just trying to help," I said. "Arvo was in trouble. We couldn't figure out any other way to do it." I looked from my dad to General Johnson. "We couldn't just leave him there–hurt and in danger. You would never abandon an injured soldier."

"It's what you always talk about," Giselle said. "Do the

215

right thing. Support the mission. We were keeping him safe. We were helping him be free. Did you think I wasn't listening to you all this time?"

"You ran away to Paris without telling anyone," General Johnson said. "Do you have any idea how dangerous that is?"

"Dad!" Giselle straightened up. "It's not the DMZ. This is Paris. People like us here."

"We didn't run away!" I said.

"It's true," Vivian added. "There was very little running. Mostly we walked." She gave the parents a little smile and got nothing back.

"Daddy," Giselle said, "he was all alone, and he needed us. He wanted all the things we want: freedom, self-determination, justice. It's what you talk about at home. It's what we sing about at church. You can't just teach me all that stuff and then expect me not to care."

Dad turned away from the table and looked me in the eye. "Do you know how hard your mother works to make music happen in your life? She's the one who thought you were ready for this trip. 'Give that girl some room to grow,' she said to me. 'Trust her,' she said."

I knew how Mom got when she was worried. Whenever we were in a crowded place in Berlin, she was terrified about the boys getting lost or stolen; she always made me hold their hands. She could work an emergency room full of gunshot wounds and even help with an amputation and totally keep her focus, but the thought of losing her own boys in a foreign country made her panic.

"I never meant to make her worry," I said. "We did all that work to come home so you wouldn't have to worry."

"You lied. You lied to both of us."

"I lied to save a man's life," I said, trying to hold my voice steady.

"You just wanted to play in that contest with your friends."

"These are the best friends I'll ever have," I said, determined not to cry. "And I'm never going to see them again."

I thought he was going to yell. Every muscle in my body was ready for it, like you get ready for a wave at the beach.

"If you had told me about Sergeant Kross five days ago, I'd have gotten him out of East Germany, no problem. If you'd told us someone stole your money, we'd have come to get you." He shook his head, looking at the ground, and I could feel the weight of his disappointment. "Are we really so hard to talk to?"

"It's not you, Dad. It's not Mom, either. I wanted to save Arvo by myself. I wanted to find my own way home."

"Jody," he said, and looked up. "I was a year younger than you when my dad died. . . . I've found my own way ever since. Everything I've gained in my life has been my own accomplishment." He shrugged the way he does. "And I'd give it all up to have my dad back. Please. I'm right here. Talk to me."

I should have hugged him. I wanted to, but all that disappointment stood between us.

"When we get to Texas," I began, "I'll try to be...less independent."

Dad sighed, took off his glasses, and rubbed his eyes. "Independence isn't a crime, you know. But we could start with something less extravagant than international espionage."

"Right!" I nodded earnestly. "I'll never help a Soviet spy escape ever again. I swear."

Dad folded his arms and looked down at me. "Exactly. I think we'll start with something much more local. How about a morning paper route?"

I was not a morning person.

"I have some serious paying back to do, don't I?"

"Oh yes."

"So I guess we better move to a town that has a newspaper then, even if it doesn't have an orchestra."

"I think I can promise that."

"Okay."

I walked over to where Vivi and her mom were talking with Giselle.

"Well, girls," Vivian's mom said briskly as the dads meandered over. "I spoke with our ambassador this afternoon. Apologies were in order for all the disruption you've caused, and he was good enough to remind me that in addition to this outrageous escapade, which has caused us considerable grief, not to mention expense..."

General Johnson nodded grimly, and my dad was right there with him.

"...you have also managed," Vivian's mom went on, "to save the life of an important intelligence contact. Something that will benefit not just our own country but the stability of the region."

Dad opened his mouth to say something, but Mrs. Armstrong held up her hand and went on. "Needless to say, medals will not be awarded. Nonetheless, the ambassador would like to express his thanks by offering us the use of a vehicle for the remainder of the afternoon."

I looked from Vivian to Giselle, hardly daring to believe it.

"This is very generous," General Johnson said. "While I am deeply disappointed by many"–he looked sternly at Giselle–"of your decisions of the last five days, your rescue and resuscitation of our Soviet contact was perfectly executed. Your subsequent actions, though ill-advised, were surprisingly effective . . . a soldier twice your age might not have done as well."

Giselle studied the ground in front of her feet, but I could see her beaming.

"So, girls," Vivi's mom said, "did you see everything you'd hoped to in Paris? We have a few hours before our flight home."

"Let's go to the Eiffel Tower," Giselle said.

"Yeah," Vivian said. "I think I want a picture of us at the top of the Eiffel Tower after all."

"Seriously?"

"Honestly, Jody," Vivian said, "we never would have come at all if you hadn't saved Arvo's life."

"You're the girl with the plan, honey," Giselle said. "We would have been lost without you."

"Eiffel Tower, it is," Mrs. Armstrong said. "I'm sure our driver can arrange a quick visit."

Apparently this is true. If you have the right kind of car, you can park anywhere and also go to the front of the elevator line. After we'd posed for serious and silly pictures at the top of the Eiffel Tower, I went a few steps away from the others and leaned on the rail looking down at the cream-colored buildings, plain and fancy, and the green fluff of treetops in the park just across the river. It was a much tidier-looking city from up there, and I wondered what would become of Arvo, and if his country would ever be free. Dad came and leaned on the rail next to me, and I thought he was going to say something, but for a long time he didn't.

"About your music," he said. "You were disqualified from the competition. Contestants have to play a published piece. I know that competition was important to you and you worked hard for months. I'm sorry it didn't turn out better."

"Oh." I looked down at the Seine and the slow, flat boats pushing people and cargo. "I guess I forgot about that. I was trying so hard to get home."

"However, you succeeded in impressing a very

distinguished panel of judges. I hear that was quite a piece of music you wrote."

"Really?"

"Really. The French judge even invited you to attend his school." Dad reached into his kit bag and pulled out my music notebook.

"You got my notebook back!" I snatched it out of his hand. It was a little bit more tattered and bent than before. I flipped it open to "Canon for Three Friends." It was still there, every page.

"Thanks." I hugged the notebook to my heart. "I need this, Dad. I can manage the new house and the new school, all of it, if I have this."

He put a hand on my shoulder. "I know," he said quietly. "I do know that about my Jo."

I rested my head on his sleeve for a second, and then we went back to leaning on the railing.

"Did you know, I had to give up my piano lessons when my dad passed," he said. "I never really missed them until now, when I see you loving music every bit as much as I did back then." He shrugged and looked out at the city of Paris. "I wish I knew how to read your composition, Jody. That'd be a thing to know. I wish I could still play."

I took that in as we stood side by side watching the river.

"Time to go, girls!" Mrs. Armstrong called from the far side of the platform.

"Aww, Mom, one last look?" Vivi came and tugged me

over to where she and Giselle were looking east toward the Latin Quarter.

"See?" Giselle said. "That dome over there is the Sorbonne, and the two square towers are Saint Sulpice, where we first played on the street."

"Hey, your notebook!" Vivi pulled it out from under my arm and flipped it open. "Can I have my part to our canon? I only got to play it once." She looked through the pages until she came to my now very wrinkled and coffee-stained song. "Can I have this? Please?" She looked at me over the tops of her glasses. "Nobody ever wrote a song just for me."

"Not this copy," I said, taking back my notebook and closing it carefully so none of the loose pages got blown away. "I'll write out your part for you," I said. "All the parts—on good paper. And I'll send it to both of you, okay?"

"So we're writing each other, then," Giselle said.

"Yeah!" Vivian said. "Of course we're writing."

"Good," Giselle went on. "None of this wimpy I-miss-you stuff and then dropping the letters when you get other friends because it's embarrassing to say I have other friends now." She gave us both the look, and I totally got what she was talking about. That had happened to me twice already.

"Of course we're going to have other friends," Giselle went on. "Good friends, I hope. But I'm never going to find girls like you. I can tell."

"Okay," I said. "I'll write."

"And one other thing," Vivian said. She and Giselle both turned away from the city sights and faced me.

"Close your eyes and hold out your hand," Giselle commanded.

She set a square package of paper in my hand. It was warm, as if it had been carried about in a pocket all day.

"What's this?"

"Open it!"

It was the song I'd written at Shakespeare and Company. The wind rattled the pages, but I held them tight.

"I promised Mr. Whitman..." I looked from Vivi to Giselle, amazed. "I left it for him in the children's room. I was going to give it to him, but it's not finished and—"

"We talked to Mr. Whitman while you were off finding the money in that book," Vivian said. "And he said we could keep your song. He doesn't even play music. Can you believe it? He was pretending."

"He said"—Giselle slumped her shoulders the way Mr. Whitman stands and tried to imitate his voice—" 'When you have a friend as tenderhearted as that one, you should remember that she will do for her friends what she is not brave enough to do for herself.'"

"So we've been thinking," Vivi said. "And we decided you can have your song if you promise to finish it."

"There is no cello part," Giselle said. "What's up with that? Finish the song and then send it to me."

"Yeah," Vivi chimed in. "Because honestly, Jody, you're the one with all the talent. You're the one who's going to be famous someday."

"I heard what Mrs. Jorgenson said about your song," Giselle said. "She's going to give you a full-ride scholarship, I know it. And then it's straight to Juilliard for you!"

"You'll have your own symphony in no time," Vivi added.

I just laughed. "Oh no, I totally have other plans." I pulled out the British agent's card and showed it to them. "I'm going to be a spymaster. Look! We're practically partners already!"

We headed for the elevator, laughing. Vivi made jokes about my becoming the girl version of James Bond, and Giselle started singing the movie theme song.

If I'd known then how hard it would be to get into music school and learn how to compose and become a working musician, I'd have left my dream right there on the top of the Eiffel Tower, where I could admire it from a comfortable distance. But I had no idea. I only knew that I was in love with music, and there were two best friends and one singing soldier in the whole world who thought I had talent, and that was all I needed.

Author's Note

One of the joys of writing fiction is revisiting favorite places. Germany is one such place for me. I lived there from 1990 to 1992 in that fascinating era just after the Berlin Wall came down. My husband, a lieutenant in the army, was stationed in Aschaffenburg in northern Bavaria, but we lived in a tiny town where I had the chance to develop friendships with my neighbors, attend community events, and practice my German. It was from my friends and neighbors and from local newspapers and radio that I learned about the impact of the fall of the Berlin Wall on German families.

After losing the Second World War in 1945, Germany was a country in ruins. Nearly every city had been bombed. More than half the population was homeless. Most German industries were completely destroyed and had to be rebuilt from the ground up. Without help, the country was in danger of falling into chaos. The allies–France, England, the Soviet Union, and the United States–worked together to rebuild Germany. They divided it into four zones, and each

Division of Germany, 1945

North Sea

Baltic Sea

DENMARK
SWEDEN
POLAND
NETHERLANDS
BELGIUM
FRANCE
SWITZERLAND
AUSTRIA
CZECHOSLOVAKIA

Hamburg
Bremen
Berlin

WEST GERMANY
EAST GERMANY

Frankfurt

Zones of Occupation

- United States
- France
- Great Britain
- Soviet Union

Berlin

West Berlin
East Berlin

0   10 miles

country helped the Germans in its zone construct homes and roads, resettle millions of refugees, and hold elections for new political leaders. Berlin had been the center of the German army command and had sustained the heaviest bombing. As the capital and as Germany's largest city, it needed the most help to recover. The allies divided Berlin into four sections, with each ally taking responsibility for one area even though the city fell well within the borders of the Soviet zone.

Britain, France, and the United States handed the responsibility for Germany back to the Germans as soon as they could function on their own. The Soviets were not eager to leave the northeast section of Germany, which they occupied. Their losses in the war were greater by far than those of the other allies, and they wanted to keep the Eastern part of Germany as a Communist country. France, Britain, and the United States refused to abandon their sectors of Berlin to the Communists, and many Germans who did not want to live under Communist rule fled to the Western sectors of Berlin. The situation became very tense, and many feared that war would break out in Germany again between the United States and the Soviet Union.

Instead of fighting, the Communists built a wall around the French, British, and American sectors of Berlin. They also built a barrier along the Soviet zone of Germany and made their occupation zone into East Germany, a Communist country that was controlled by the much more powerful

Soviet Union. They posted guards along the Wall with orders to shoot and kill any person trying to cross to the Western side. Over the twenty-eight years that the Wall stood, nearly two hundred people died trying to cross. Many were shot. Some drowned trying to swim across the border, and others suffocated in collapsed tunnels. It was possible for West Germans to travel to the East, but they had to have special paperwork and pass through a checkpoint, where their cars were searched to prevent people from escaping. One such border crossing was called Checkpoint Charlie.

After more than forty years of suffering under Communist domination, the East Germans began to protest their government in an organized and peaceful way. In the past, protesters had been arrested. But now the protests grew so large that there was not a prison in the entire country that could hold the marchers. Other Communist countries in Eastern Europe were also organizing and electing new leadership. When Hungary and Czechoslovakia opened their borders, thousands of East Germans flooded through them and into West Germany, abandoning everything they owned for a chance to move to the West. Soon there were not enough workers to run factories. Teachers abandoned their classrooms. Doctors left their hospitals. The whole world watched as thousands of East Germans took to the streets, marching and singing, using many of the tactics Americans had used in the civil rights movement. In the end, the East German government reluctantly agreed to hold elections and open the borders.

The result was an outpouring of joy. Thousands of Germans rushed to the Wall, East Germans to escape and West Germans to welcome their long-lost countrymen with open arms. People sang and danced in the streets; they shared gifts of candy and champagne. Hundreds of elated Berliners helped bring the Wall down with their own hammers and chisels.

Berlin was a city in transition for all of 1990. The Berlin Wall first opened on November 9, 1989, but the Wall was massive. It ran for twenty-eight miles through the city and in places was thick enough for a half dozen people to stand shoulder to shoulder on top. It was made of concrete, steel, and barbed wire, so it took many months of work with heavy machinery to dismantle. In writing my story, I chose not to chase down the exact dates when sections of the Wall were torn down. I attempted to convey a city and a culture in transition, both proud of the defeat of Communism and apprehensive about the daunting restoration ahead.

The plight of Soviet soldiers in this era was particularly striking. After their war in Afghanistan, which was as difficult and divisive for them as Vietnam was for the United States, Soviet soldiers suffered from a failing Soviet economy. They were often not paid and were always undersupplied. Corruption was rampant, and the hazing of enlisted men was distressingly common. Although Arvo is my own invention, his difficulties were shared by thousands of non-Russian soldiers who served in the Soviet army.

The commitment of citizens in Estonia, and its neighbors Latvia and Lithuania, to peaceful separation from the Soviet Union was impressive. Once the Communists let go of their strict control of newspapers and television, Estonians and citizens of the other Baltic states were able to learn the truth about their oppression and organize large-scale protests. Vocal music is a cornerstone of Estonian culture. The people gather every summer for song festivals with choirs that number in the thousands. There are more folk songs written in Estonian than in any other language in the world. In 1988 at their song festival grounds, more than three hundred thousand Estonians, about a third of the entire population, decided to risk imprisonment, or worse, to sing a song—their national anthem. To everyone's amazement, three hundred thousand people singing was intimidating to the Soviets in a way that armed resistance was not. Physical force is easily met with greater physical force. The solidarity the Estonians expressed by singing together proved very difficult for the Soviets to fight. Decades earlier, Martin Luther King Jr. had called this tactic "meeting physical force with soul force."

Estonia and its neighbors Lithuania and Latvia gained their independence in August 1991, just a year after my story takes place.

* * *

The one character in this story who is not my invention is George Whitman, the owner of the Shakespeare and Company bookshop in Paris. He ran the shop for decades as a combination store, literary salon, and refuge for down-and-out writers. At the time of this writing, Mr. Whitman is in his nineties and still living above the shop, while the day-to-day operations of the bookstore are run by his daughter, Sylvia. I had the pleasure of visiting Shakespeare and Company in the fall of 1991 and found it a book lover's paradise. The other sights the girls visited in Paris are all still there, and you can trace their path on any map of the city.

You will find no trace of the shabbiness the girls found on Unter den Linden in Berlin today. With a typical mixture of hard work, sacrifice, and more than a little angst, a united Germany has completely renovated the border area around the Brandenburg Gate. The former site of the Berlin Wall is now home to new streets, museums, fine dining and shopping, and a memorial to victims of the Holocaust. The places the girls visited in Berlin are reasonably historically accurate given the pace of change in 1990, but I took some liberties in my story with the location of the railroad bridge and the character of the landscape along the Spree River.

Although I have not been to Europe in many years, I treasured the opportunity to live there and hope to return someday. I also hope that you will learn foreign languages and travel abroad, just as Jody and her friends did. Please do tell your parents before you go!

Acknowledgments

Thank you to my own trio for making music with me. Your patience and persistence have reawakened a joy I'd long forgotten—a joy without which this story would never have taken shape.

About the Author

Rosanne Parry moved to Germany in the spring of 1990, just as the Berlin Wall was coming down. She ran away to Paris for one glorious weekend with her soldier husband, firstborn baby, and an enormous purple stroller. The three of them are best friends to this day. Rosanne is the author of *Heart of a Shepherd*, which has been honored as a *Washington Post* Best Kids' Book of the Year, a *Kirkus Reviews* Best Children's Book of the Year, and a *Horn Book* Fanfare Best Book of the Year. She also plays the violin, for which she has never been honored with a prize of any kind. She now lives with her husband in an old farmhouse in Portland, Oregon, where they raise four children, three chickens, five kinds of fruit, and their voices in the occasional song. Visit Rosanne at rosanneparry.com.

YEARLING!

Looking for more great books to read?
Check these out!

- ❑ *All-of-a-Kind Family* by Sydney Taylor
- ❑ *Are You There God? It's Me, Margaret* by Judy Blume
- ❑ *Blubber* by Judy Blume
- ❑ *The City of Ember* by Jeanne DuPrau
- ❑ *Crash* by Jerry Spinelli
- ❑ *The Girl Who Threw Butterflies* by Mick Cochrane
- ❑ *The Gypsy Game* by Zilpha Keatley Snyder
- ❑ *Heart of a Shepherd* by Rosanne Parry
- ❑ *The King of Mulberry Street* by Donna Jo Napoli
- ❑ *The Mailbox* by Audrey Shafer
- ❑ *Me, Mop, and the Moondance Kid* by Walter Dean Myers
- ❑ *My One Hundred Adventures* by Polly Horvath
- ❑ *The Penderwicks* by Jeanne Birdsall
- ❑ *Skellig* by David Almond
- ❑ *Soft Rain* by Cornelia Cornelissen
- ❑ *Stealing Freedom* by Elisa Carbone
- ❑ *Toys Go Out* by Emily Jenkins
- ❑ *A Traitor Among the Boys* by Phyllis Reynolds Naylor
- ❑ *Two Hot Dogs with Everything* by Paul Haven
- ❑ *When My Name Was Keoko* by Linda Sue Park

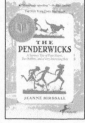

Visit **www.randomhouse.com/kids** for additional reading suggestions
in fantasy, adventure, mystery, and humor!